Why couldn't she just relax and accept his protection?

But she couldn't relax around him. The memory of their time together was too potent, the attraction between them still far too dynamic.

She got out of the truck and watched as Dakota removed their daughter from her car seat. The baby dropped her head to his shoulder as if it were natural for this cowboy with a smile that matched her own to be carrying her into the house.

Viviana hurried to unlock the door. She noticed the doll almost at once, at the edge of the walkway next to a flowerpot. It wasn't her daughter's.

Apprehension made her palms clammy as she stooped to pick it up. The back of the doll's head had been crushed. Fake blood dripped down the collar of the dress.

She started to slam it back to the walk and spotted a square of paper tucked inside the clothing. As she read it, the words blurred. Her hands began to shake. And then she felt the earth moving beneath her feet and the walkway rushing to her face....

JOANNA WAYNE

COWBOY FEVER

TORONTO NEW YORK LONDON
AMSTERDAM PARIS SYDNEY HAMBURG
STOCKHOLM ATHENS TOKYO MILAN MADRID
PRAGUE WARSAW BUDAPEST AUCKLAND

To our good friends the Mitchells. Always nice to have you two around to catch a movie with when I need a break from the computer. And a hug to Wayne for enduring my deadlines.

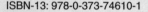

Recycling programs for this product may not exist in your area.

ISBN-13: 978-0-373-74610-1

COWBOY FEVER

Copyright © 2011 by Jo Ann Vest

This edition published by arrangement with Harlequin Books S.A.

For questions and comments about the quality of this book please contact us at Customer_eCare@Harlequin.ca.

® and TM are trademarks of the publisher. Trademarks indicated with ® are registered in the United States Patent and Trademark Office, the Canadian Trade Marks Office and in other countries.

www.Harlequin.com

Printed in U.S.A.

ABOUT THE AUTHOR

Joanna Wayne was born and raised in Shreveport, Louisiana, and received her undergraduate and graduate degrees from LSU-Shreveport. She moved to New Orleans in 1984, and it was there that she attended her first writing class and joined her first professional writing organization. Her debut novel, *Deep in the Bayou,* was published in 1994.

Now, dozens of published books later, Joanna has made a name for herself as being on the cutting edge of romantic suspense in both series and single-title novels. She has been on the Waldenbooks bestseller list for romance and has won many industry awards. She is also a popular speaker at writing organizations and local community functions and has taught creative writing at the University of New Orleans Metropolitan College.

Joanna currently resides in a small community forty miles north of Houston, Texas, with her husband. Though she still has many family and emotional ties to Louisiana, she loves living in the Lone Star State. You may write Joanna at P.O. Box 852, Montgomery, Texas 77356.

Books by Joanna Wayne

HARLEQUIN INTRIGUE
955—MAVERICK CHRISTMAS
975—24/7
1001—24 KARAT AMMUNITION*
1019—TEXAS GUN SMOKE*
1041—POINT BLANK PROTECTOR*
1065—LOADED*
1096—MIRACLE AT COLTS RUN CROSS*
1123—COWBOY COMMANDO‡
1152—COWBOY TO THE CORE‡
1167—BRAVO, TANGO, COWBOY‡
1195—COWBOY DELIRIUM*‡
1228—COWBOY SWAGGER†
1249—GENUINE COWBOY†
1264—AK-COWBOY†
1289—COWBOY FEVER†

*Four Brothers of Colts Run Cross
‡Special Ops Texas
†Sons of Troy Ledger

CAST OF CHARACTERS

Viviana Mancini—Beautiful Emergency Room doctor in danger for merely doing her job.

Dakota Ledger—Gutsy, sexy bull rider with a past that threatens his future. Youngest son of Troy Ledger.

Briana Ledger—Viviana's seven-month-old daughter.

Claire Evers—Nanny who takes care of Briana while Viviana is on duty at the hospital.

Troy Ledger—Dakota's father who has more reasons than proving his innocence to be obsessed with finding his wife's killer.

Helene Ledger—Murdered when Dakota was only six years old. Superstition has it that her ghost still haunts the old ranch house hoping for her sons to come home or perhaps seeking justice for her own death.

Dylan, Sean, Travis and Wyatt Ledger—The other four sons of Troy Ledger

Collette, Eve and Julie Ledger—Wives to Dylan, Sean and Travis.

Detective Harry Cortez—Homicide detective better known as Dirty Harry. He does whatever it takes to solve his case.

Gordon Miles—Detective who takes over for Harry Cortez.

Kevin Lucas—Dies of gunshot wound in the Emergency Room.

Shelby Lucas—Kevin's sister.

Hank Bateman—Threatens to kill Viviana if she testifies against him.

George Bateman—Hank's brother who was once imprisoned with Troy Ledger.

Nick Jefferson—Attorney with the D.A.'s.

Melody Hollister—Nick Jefferson's assistant.

Chapter One

Dakota Ledger was back in Texas and the heat was on. Sweat rolled down his back and pooled at his armpits, staining his lucky red Western shirt. The smell of livestock and manure permeated the still air. "All My Ex's Live in Texas" blared from an aging sound system. The edgy excitement of competition was electric in the stifling June air.

"Gotta love bull riding in San Antonio."

Dakota turned to the youthful cowboy who was grinning like a puppy with a new bone. "What's so special about San Antonio?" Dakota asked.

"I qualified for the competition."

"That'll do it."

Dakota didn't know the rider's real name, but even though he was relatively new to the Professional Bull Riders Association circuit, he'd already earned a nickname. "Cockroach" stemmed from the way he scurried out of the reach of a bull's kicking hooves. It was a great talent to have if you wanted to keep living with all parts working.

Cockroach rubbed his palms against his chaps. "This is my first year to compete in PBR-sanctioned events, so I'm a little nervous."

"The adrenaline will take care of that once you drop onto the bull's back."

"I'm counting on that." Cockroach adjusted his hat. "One day I hope to be the PBRA world champion, just like you were two years ago. A million-dollar purse. I could use that. Not to mention all those endorsements you have."

"Bull riding's not about the money."

"I know." Cockroach toed the dirt as if putting out a cigarette. "It's a long, hard ride from the bottom to the top, but I plan to be one of the few who make it."

"Persistence is a large part of the battle," Dakota agreed.

"And skill is the rest," Cockroach said.

"Skill, passion and luck," Dakota corrected.

"You gotta love what you're doing. And you gotta stay alive to keep doing it."

Cockroach reached down and adjusted his right spur. "Have you ever been seriously hurt?"

"Never met a bull rider who hasn't. I've had cracked ribs, concussions, a broken right wrist and bruises probably on every inch of my body."

"Hey, Dakota. Looking good."

Dakota turned toward the railing that separated the paid attendees from the competitors. A group of young women were leaning over the railing, probably not a one of them over twenty years old. Not that he was all that much older at twenty-five, but he sure felt it.

Still, he tipped his hat and smiled.

"Your friend's cute, too," one of the females called.

Cockroach beamed, turned a tad red and tipped his hat to his vocal admirer.

"What's your favorite rodeo town?" Cockroach asked when he turned back to Dakota.

Dakota nudged his worn Stetson back from his forehead. It damn sure wasn't San Antonio or any other town within five hundred miles of here, but he wasn't getting into that.

"Doesn't really matter where you are. It always comes down to just you, the bull and the clock."

"Can't be the same in places like Montana. I mean look at those hot babes over there. Short shorts, halter tops, sun-streaked hair and all that luscious tanned flesh. Bet you don't get that in cold country."

"They've got hot buckle bunnies every place they've got rodeo competitions," Dakota assured him. "The names change. The flirting and seduction games remain the same."

At least that had been true for him until he'd run into a certain dark-haired beauty with class and brains after a bull got the best of him last year at Rodeo Houston. The attraction between them had struck like lightning, shooting sparks without warning. They'd had six days together before he'd had to move on to the next competition. Six torrid, exciting, fantastic days.

End of story. He hadn't been the one to write the finale. The rejection had stung a lot more than expected. His performance level had taken a drastic drop for several months after that. He could thank Viviana—along with a couple of injuries—that he didn't even make it to the championship finals last year.

Dakota turned back to the circle of dirt where he'd face tonight's battle. Letting anything interfere with your concentration was suicide for a bull rider.

Which was why he should have never come back to Texas. Even before he'd met Viviana, the odds here were stacked against him. The Ledger name was infamous in the Lone Star State and that had nothing to do with his reputation with the bulls.

Nineteen years after the fact, the brutal murder of Dakota's mother was still being written and talked about in this area of Texas. She'd been shot at home, in a ranch house less than a hundred miles from where he stood right now.

His father, Troy, had been convicted of the crime. Dakota had been six years old at the time.

Luckily, questions about his past hadn't come up today in his interviews with the local media. All they'd focused on was taking pictures and asking him about his success. He suspected that was because the competition's organizers had told them any mention of Troy Ledger was off-limits.

Cockroach got the signal to head toward the chute. He looked over to the female cheering squad and tipped his hat before swaggering toward the bucking, snorting beast that was already fighting to clear the chute.

"Remember, it's just you and the bull," Dakota shouted after him. Six seconds into the ride, the bull bucked and veered to the left. Cockroach was thrown off. Fortunately, it was his hat and not his head that got entangled with the bull's hooves. True to his nickname, the cowboy got out of the way while Jim Angle distracted the indignant animal.

Jim was one of the rodeo clown greats. It had been Jim Angle who'd saved Dakota from getting seriously injured back in Houston the night he'd met Viviana. The past attacked again, this time so strong Dakota couldn't shut the memories down.

Images of Viviana filled his head. Dark, curly hair that fell to her slender shoulders. Full, sensual lips. Eyes a man could drown in. A touch that had set him on fire.

Damn. If he didn't clear his mind, he'd never hang on for the full eight seconds, and he needed a good showing tonight to make it to the final round in this event tomorrow. A rider couldn't rest on past laurels and the competition got tougher every year.

He'd drawn the meanest of the rough stock tonight. That was half the battle to getting a high score. The other half was up to Dakota.

He was the last rider of the evening and he worked to psyche himself up as the other contenders got their shot at racking up points. As his turn drew near, he fit the leather glove on his riding hand and one of the other riders helped him tape it in place. The resin came next, just enough to improve his grip. Then he climbed onto the chute. It was time for action.

A rush of adrenaline shot through him as he gripped his worn and trusty bull rope and felt the 1700-pound bull buck beneath him. It would be a hell of a ride. The crowd was with him. Their cheers pounded in his head, their voices an indistinguishable roar.

"Hey, Ledger. We don't like murderers around here."

Unlike the cheers, the taunt was distinct. Cutting. Jagged.

The gate clanked open and Devil's Deed charged from the chute.

In what seemed like a heartbeat, the bull went into a belly roll and Dakota went sailing through the air. His right shoulder ground into the hard earth. A kicking hoof collided with his ribs as he tried to scramble to safety.

Pain shot through him like a bullet.

Yep. He was home.

Chapter Two

"STAT. Ambulance en route."

Dr. Mancini looked up at the male E.R. nurse delivering the news.

"And I so needed this cup of coffee."

"I know. It's been murder in here tonight. Must be the full moon."

"More likely that I volunteered to pull Dr. Cairn's shift for her." She took a large gulp of the much-needed caffeine. "Nature of the emergency?" she asked, shifting her brain to work mode.

"Gunshot wound to the head. Critical blood loss. Vitals at life-threatening levels. "

There went her last chance of getting home on time and relieving the nanny tonight. "Any other details?"

"Caucasian male, likely early twenties, picked up in the back parking lot of a bar in the downtown area. Expected arrival…" He glanced at his watch. "Any minute."

"Alert the nurse assigned to the shock trauma center and also Dr. Evans."

"I'm on it."

She was glad Dan Evans was on duty tonight. He was one of the top neurosurgeons in Texas. "Also alert the O.R.," she called to the departing nurse.

Fatigue was forgotten as she hurried down the halls to the trauma unit. They'd already lost one patient tonight. Hopefully, they'd save this one.

"Dr. Mancini."

She recognized the voice. Police Detective Harry Cortez, or Dirty Harry, as she'd come to think of him. Not because of his toughness—though she expected he was plenty tough—but because the front of his shirt always bore testimony to his latest meal.

"If you're here about the patient with the gunshot wound, you'll have to wait. I haven't seen him as yet."

His eyes narrowed. "You have a patient with a gunshot wound?"

"Arriving as we speak, but don't even think about questioning him until I give you clearance. This is a hospital, not the police station."

"I'm only doing my job, just like you, Doctor. Besides, I'm here to talk to you about Hank Bateman."

Mention of the name filled her with disgust. "We'll have to talk later."

The squeak of a gurney's wheels came from near the E.R. entrance. She raced toward the trauma center. The slap of the detective's street shoes on the tiled floor signaled he was right behind her.

She was sliding her long fingers into a pair of sterile gloves when she heard the detective's voice outside the examining room.

"Who shot you? C'mon. Name the bastard. He won't come after you again. I'll see to it. Just give me the name."

She walked to the door as the patient was rolled in. She shot a stern warning look at Cortez, and he waved in surrender and backed away.

One look at the patient and her stomach rolled. She should be desensitized by now, but the sight of bloody tissue oozing from the skull was not the kind of thing she'd ever get used to. The victim's chance of survival was next to zero. The miracle was that he had lived to make it to the hospital.

The young man coughed, and blood mixed with spittle spilled from his lips. His mouth kept moving. He was trying to say something. She leaned in close, but the gurgled murmurings were too garbled to understand.

"I'm Dr. Mancini," she said as she helped the nurse get him hooked up to the heart monitor. "I'll try to ease your pain."

"And I'm Dr. Evans," the young neurosurgeon said as he joined them.

The patient coughed again, this time choking on the blood.

"Shhh… Shell…"

She leaned in close. "Are you trying to tell me who shot you?"

Before he could nod or mumble a reply, the line on the monitor went flat.

"EITHER YOU GO TO the emergency room by ambulance or I drive you," Jim Angle said.

Dakota shrugged, but winced as he tried to grab a gulp of bracing air. "I don't need to see a doctor. It's just a contusion."

"You don't know that."

"I was wearing my protective vest."

"You could still have a few cracked ribs. Butch Cobb was wearing a vest in Phoenix."

All the riders knew about Butch. He'd been one of the best until a fractured rib had punctured his right lung. "A freak accident," Dakota said.

He lifted a bottle of water to his mouth. His chest protested the movement with such vengeance that he grimaced.

Naturally, Jim noticed.

"You need to be x-rayed."

"I needed to stay on that bull eight seconds."

"You don't always have to play the tough guy, Dakota."

"Who's playing? But if it makes you happy, I'll stop by the emergency room, old man, and get checked out."

"Watch who you're calling 'old man' or I'll toss you over my shoulder and haul your sorry ass to the hospital."

"How about you just collect my bull rope and glove for me?"

"Can do, and then I'm driving you to the hospital."

"Just what I need, a chauffeur in rodeo-clown makeup."

What Dakota wanted was a couple of pain-killers, a six-pack and a soft bed, but he knew that Jim was right. He should get the injury checked out. If it was something serious, the faster he got it tended to, the better off he'd be.

The nearest hospital was only a ten-minute drive. He'd passed it on his way to the arena tonight. He could easily drive himself. He started unbuttoning his shirt. He had a clean one in his truck and he didn't want the hospital deciding they had to rip this one off of him.

He almost doubled over from a stab of pain as he shrugged out of the shirt. His chest felt like someone had just whacked it with a two-by-four.

"Get in," Jim said.

This time Dakota didn't argue.

Chapter Three

"We still need to talk, Dr. Mancini."

Drats. The detective was still here. She adjusted the strap on her handbag. The nagging headache that had begun at her first sight of the dying gunshot victim intensified sharply.

"Do we have to talk tonight? I was just leaving."

He nodded. "It's important."

What wasn't? "There's a small conference room at the end of the hall," she said. "But can we make this short? It's been crazy around here tonight, and I'm exhausted."

A tinge of guilt settled in her chest. She had no right to complain about exhaustion when, unlike two of the night's patients, she was alive.

Detective Cortez followed her to the conference room, which was little more than a large supply cabinet with chairs and a small round table instead of shelves. She perched on the edge of one of the chairs.

Cortez scratched the back of his head and dandruff snowed onto the collar of his dark cotton sport shirt. "We have some complications."

"Don't tell me they've postponed the Bateman trial?"

"No, but Judge Carter was relieved of the case."

"Why?"

"His wife's been diagnosed with cancer and he's taking an emergency leave from the bench."

"Won't they just appoint a new judge?"

"They have," Cortez said. "It's Judge Nelson."

"Mary Lester Nelson?"

"That's the one," Cortez said.

"You don't sound too happy about the change."

"Judge Nelson has a reputation for being soft on rotten sons of bitches like Hank Bateman. Pardon my French."

"Surely she won't let a child killer off with a slap on the wrist."

"No, she'll throw in a little community service." Sarcasm punctuated his voice. "She already decided his rights were being denied and set bail this afternoon. I'm sure Bateman is out walking the streets by now."

"Doesn't she know what happened three months ago when Judge Carter decided that the prosecution was requesting unreasonable extensions and he decided bail was in order?"

"I'm sure the prosecution made certain she knew Bateman made a run for the border."

"Not just made a run for it, he was crossing it when Border Patrol made the arrest and sent him back to jail," she said. "And still Judge Nelson released a child killer on bail. The more I learn about the justice system, the more unjust I think it is."

"At this point, Bateman is just an *alleged* child killer. His attorney is insisting he's innocent."

"But we know he isn't. He admitted that he'd been with his girlfriend's baby all evening the night the infant died."

"Yeah. Nice guy. Babysitting for the woman who's out turning tricks to buy him crack cocaine."

"I don't give a—" She threw up her hands.

"This isn't about the mother. It's about getting justice for a helpless infant. And our evidence is indisputable."

"Until a defense attorney starts whittling away at it."

"There is nothing to whittle." Her irritation was building so fast, she couldn't contain it. "There was excessive retinal hemorrhaging, and bruising on the baby's arms and stomach that was not consistent with a fall. That infant died from NAT."

"Calm down," Cortez said. "You don't have to convince me the cause of death was non-accidental trauma delivered by a heartless bastard. I don't doubt the autopsy findings. But jurors aren't always swayed by printed reports. They react to emotion. That's why I'm counting on your testimony."

"And nothing will stop me from appearing at that trial."

"Good."

"So what is this visit really about?"

"Now that Bateman's out of jail there's a good chance he'll try to contact you himself."

"To try to frighten me into refusing to testify?"

Cortez nodded.

"It won't work, Detective, no more than his threatening notes have or last month's visit from his thug friend who showed up in the E.R. pretending to be ill."

"The trial is only nine days away. Bateman will be getting desperate. He may up the ante."

The tone of the detective's voice alarmed her. "Surely you don't think I'm in any kind of danger."

"I just think you should be careful. If you so much as see him hanging around or get a phone call from him, I want to know about it. There's a chance I could take that information to the judge and get the bail decision reversed. Having Bateman behind bars is our only assurance that he won't skip the country and hide out in some remote area of Mexico."

So it wasn't her that the detective was worried about. But she was as interested in seeing Hank Bateman behind bars as he was—permanently locked away, where he could never harm another helpless infant.

But she had other concerns, as well. "I have a seven-month-old daughter. I can't have her in danger."

"She won't be. Neither will you. I'll see to

that." Cortez pulled a business card from his shirt pocket and dropped it onto the table in front of her. "Keep this with you. Call me on my cell if Bateman tries to make any type of contact with you."

She picked up the card and quickly committed the number to memory. Fortunately, that came easy for her. It was what got her through med school when she was too crushed by her mother's death to cram for finals.

They finished the conversation quickly. By the time she was ready to leave, her mind was back on the gunshot victim she hadn't been able to help.

He was young, someone's son, maybe even someone's husband or father. He'd never make it home tonight, and their lives would never be the same without him.

She'd majored in emergency medicine because she liked saving lives. More often than not, she did. But even one life needlessly lost to violence was too many.

Her car was parked about a hundred yards from the E.R. exit nearest the ambulance entrance. The back parking lot was almost deserted this time of night. An uneasy feeling skirted her senses, probably due to too much talk of Hank Bateman. She scanned the area. All was quiet.

When she reached the shiny black Acura that she'd purchased just last week, she pulled her keys from her handbag and unlocked the door. She was about to slide in when she sensed movement to her left.

"Get in."

A man grabbed her left arm and shoved what felt like the barrel of a pistol into her side. Panic seized her, crippling her reflexes, deadening her senses. She was about to slide into the seat submissively when her survival instincts kicked in.

If she got into the car with this brute, she might never escape alive.

Her former self-defense instructor's words came back to her in fragmented pieces. *Use what you have. Cause a scene. Fight for your life.*

"Get in, bitch. Do what I say so that I don't have to use this gun."

"If it's money you want…" She slung her purse at his gun hand as she frantically fit the metal car key between her fingers, fashioning a weapon of sorts.

He shoved her. She fell forward, no longer

feeling the force of the gun. She punched the man, aiming for his left eye. The metal end twisted as it buried in his eye socket.

He yelled and flailed, blindly knocking the keys from her hand. She hit the pavement running.

She was almost back to the walkway when the heel of her shoe caught on a strip of uneven pavement. Her foot came out of it and she pitched forward, her right wrist twisting beneath her as she tried to catch herself.

She heard the squeal of a car as it sped away. *Please let it be the gunman.*

But a hand touched her right shoulder. Horror reached deep inside her and she threw back her head and screamed.

The guy backed off. "Is there a problem?"

The voice echoed through her mind. Familiar. Haunting. She started to shake. Heart hammering in her chest, she turned and looked at the man standing over her.

"I didn't mean to frighten you. I heard a yell and then spotted you running across the parking lot."

Her heart skipped erratically as she studied the man who'd come to her rescue. The same depths to the dark eyes she remembered so well. The same thick, unruly hair. Even the same worn Stetson—or one exactly like it.

He stared at her as if she were a ghost.

Her heart turned inside out.

"Dakota." It was the only word she could manage without totally falling apart.

Chapter Four

"Viviana." Dakota muttered her name and stared at the woman who'd haunted so many of his dreams. He was reeling, so stunned at seeing her that he had trouble getting his mind around what had just happened or even why he was here. His memory was jolted by a dizzying stab of pain when he reached to pick up her shoe.

"Who let the bulls out?"

Jim arrived on the scene with his usual rodeo flair, still in his trademark oversize red-and-black jersey and loose shorts. A bit of the clown makeup was still smeared around his eyes, though he'd wiped it off as best he could on the way over with his dirt-smeared bandana.

Viviana stiffened and her eyes signaled an increased anxiety level. "Who are you?"

"He's a friend of mine," Dakota said quickly. "We were driving to the E.R. entrance when we heard the commotion and I spotted you racing across the parking lot." Dakota did a second visual scan of the area. There was no sign of trouble now, yet she'd screamed hysterically when he'd knelt beside her. And a car had just burned rubber leaving the lot.

"Name's Jim Angle," Jim said.

"I'm Dr. Mancini."

Dakota steadied while she slid her foot back into her shoe. It was all he could do not to pull her into his arms and hold her tight. But too many months apart and the lingering sting of rejection made him hold back. Not to mention that it would start a barrage of questions from Jim.

"What just happened out here?" Dakota asked. "Were you attacked?"

"I was leaving work. When I got to my car, a man appeared from out of nowhere and pointed a pistol at me. He told me to get in."

"Then what?" Jim asked when she stopped talking and started looking around the parking area.

"I threw my purse at him, punched him and started running."

"You must have delivered one hell of a blow," Jim said. "Man yelped like you'd gutted him. That's actually what got our attention."

"I rammed my key into his eyeball."

Jim grinned. "A woman after my heart."

She hugged her arms around her chest and shivered in spite of the warm summer air. Her gaze turned to the parking lot. "My car is gone. It was parked next to that SUV near the ambulance entrance."

"Cars are replaceable," Dakota said. She could have been killed. If he ever got his hands on the thug…

"Did you know the yellow-bellied bastard?" Jim asked.

"I've never seen the man before, at least not that I remember. A lot of patients come through the E.R."

Dakota struggled to get his head around the emotions bucking inside him. In the best of circumstances, running into Viviana so unexpectedly would have been enough to throw him off his game.

Finally, he let his eyes meet hers. "Are you sure you're okay?"

"I am now. I think you may have frightened off the gunman, except that I guess what he really wanted was cash and my car. Now he has both."

"Then lucky I made a wrong turn and came in the ambulance entrance," Jim said.

Dakota scanned the area again. "Don't you have security around here?"

"Yes, but they can't be everywhere at once."

"They could see you to your car when you leave in the wee hours of the morning."

"I've never had any trouble before. This is normally a safe area."

"Security can't do anything now," Jim said. "Call the cops. They may be able to find the low-down thief before he clears the area."

"My phone is in my purse and I hurled that at the attacker. No doubt he took it with him."

"Most likely," Dakota agreed. "But we'll check.

"I'll take a look," Jim said.

"Where are your keys?" Dakota asked.

"I'm not sure. They may have fallen to the

floor of the car, or I may have just dropped them in my panic."

Which meant the attacker could have her keys and possibly her purse with her ID. If so, he'd know where she lived.

Dakota's muscles clenched. He took his cell phone from his pocket and handed it to Viviana.

Only instead of punching in 911, she made a call to a Detective Harry Cortez. Her conversation with the man was brief and to the point. Yet, he couldn't help but wonder if her relationship with the man was business or pleasure.

By the time she finished the call, Jim had returned with her purse. "You're in luck," he said. "The purse was lying next to another parked car. Your keys were a few feet away. Guess he hotwired the vehicle."

She took the bag from him. "Good. At least he doesn't have my keys and personal information."

"What do you keep in the glove compartment?" Dakota asked.

"Usually the car registration, but I just bought this car and all of the paperwork is in my house."

"Is your detective friend coming over to investigate the situation?" Dakota asked as she returned the phone to him.

"Dirty Harry is not exactly a friend, but, yes, he's on his way. He won't be long. He just left the hospital a few minutes ago."

Dirty Harry. He must be some tough cop. But what did she mean by "not exactly a friend"? That could mean anything. A mosquito buzzed around Dakota's head. He reached up to slap it away, and his ribs screamed as if he'd leaned over a flame. He winced and struggled for a shallow breath.

"You're hurt," Viviana said.

"It's nothing."

She shook her head as if to clear it, and her dark hair danced about her slender shoulders. "If it were nothing, you wouldn't be at the hospital. What's wrong?"

"He tangled with a maniacal bull, and the bull won," Jim answered for him. "Don't happen often. This here's one of the top bull riders in the world, and he's got the buckle and the trophy to prove it."

She looked up at him, a silvery strand of moonlight glimmering in her seductive eyes.

The little emotional control he still possessed cratered.

"So you're still bull riding?" she said.

"It's in my blood. And you're still tending the sick and wounded."

"Guess that's in my blood. And now you're one of the wounded again."

"Yep." He did his best to fake a nonchalance that didn't match the heated memories boiling inside him. "Guess you could say we're right back where we started."

"Not quite, Dakota."

Crazy the way his name sounded different when she said it. Softer. Warmer. A bit gut-wrenching.

Jim's brows arched and he rocked back on the heels of his boots. "Am I missing something here? Do you two know each other?"

"Old friends," Dakota said.

"Well, damn. Why didn't you say so?"

"Just hadn't gotten around to it yet."

"What type of injury did you sustain?" Viviana asked, seamlessly snapping back into her physician role.

She acted as if they were nothing more than old friends. If he were smart, he'd treat this encounter the same way.

He tried for a deep breath and managed a shallow, excruciating one. "I took the bull's back hooves to the chest. I was wearing a safety vest, so chances are I just got bruised up a bit. I'm mostly here to get Jim off my case."

"You're obviously in distress. You need X-rays and possibly an MRI. Let me use your phone again. I'll call for a wheelchair."

"I don't need a wheelchair. I ran over here and rescued you, didn't I?"

"Give it up, Dakota." She reached for his phone. "If you weren't in severe pain and afraid something was broken, dislocated or crushed, you wouldn't be at the hospital."

"Yep, she knows you," Jim said.

While she was making the call, a small truck with a red flashing light on the roof slowly rounded the back of the building.

"Security," Viviana said, waving them over. "I'll handle this, but not until you're checked into the E.R."

Viviana told the men her car had been stolen but that she'd already called the SAPD. The next thing Dakota knew he was being rolled toward an open hospital door and a uniformed nurse was ushering him inside. Once behind the curtained cubicle, he answered a few questions and admitted that on a scale of one through ten, his pain was pushing eight.

An injection of painkiller took that down quickly, but floating in a med-induced state made it doubly hard to keep his mind off Viviana. She could have been killed.

And she might still be in danger.

It was a piss-poor time for him to be beaten up like this. Not only was he practically useless to Viviana, but in mere hours, he also had another rendezvous with a bull.

THREE HOURS LATER, Viviana stood in the hallway, poring over Dakota's test results. There was a partial tearing of the ligaments in the glenohumeral joint in his right shoulder. That would need time to heal.

There was also swelling and extensive bruising around the ribs but no serious breaks, thanks to the safety vest that he hadn't been wearing sixteen months ago when she'd first nursed him back to health. The contusions to the chest wall were making breathing and movement painful.

But what could a man expect when he made a living riding bulls?

She couldn't begin to understand his passion for danger. Couldn't make sense of his need to push his body to such physical extremes. Couldn't comprehend his willingness to put his life on the line for a rush of adrenaline and a few seconds of glory.

But, like his loner ways and his nomadic lifestyle, it was who he was. A cowboy at heart. A bull rider by choice. A man who had no desire to settle down. He'd never pretended to be anything different.

She'd accepted that months before and she wouldn't let herself start second-guessing what she knew to be true.

Betsy, the nurse who'd been assigned to Dakota, stopped at Viviana's elbow. "The cowboy in room five is gorgeous, but headstrong. He refused the offer of more pain meds, says he needs to be alert enough to drive. He's also refusing to wear the sling and says he is not about to stay overnight for observation."

"I'll talk to him."

Viviana braced herself for the emotional strain of being near Dakota and marched into room five, hugging his chart to her chest.

Dakota propped himself up a few inches

with his elbows when she entered, wincing at the pain. He was going to be seriously sore for several days.

"What's the verdict?" he asked.

As she explained the findings, he maintained a poker face. He'd heard it all before, probably more times than he could count.

"You were lucky," she said. "You could have seriously fractured bones and had a completely dislocated right shoulder…if not worse."

"Luck's the name of the game."

"In here, the name of the game is survival. I think you should be admitted for observation."

"To make certain I don't get much sleep for what's left of the night and that I'll be awakened at seven for dry eggs and cold coffee?"

"So that we can manage your pain and the respiratory therapist can see you in the morning."

"I know the routine, Doc. Deep-breathing exercises to make certain I don't develop pneumonia."

"It is important."

"I know." He took a deep breath to show her he could do it.

She managed a smile. "You do seem to have that down."

"I had a great doctor once. She taught me lots of things I haven't forgotten." His eyes said what his words only hinted at.

Tension escalated in the small cubicle until her own breathing was difficult. Nothing about dealing with Dakota had ever been easy. Their relationship had been fire and ice, passion and agony, love and…

Loss. And she couldn't go through that again, especially now.

"You need to stay off the bulls for a few days to give your body time to heal. You need ice on the injured areas, several times a day, and I recommend that you keep that right arm in a sling for the next week to give it some extra support."

"Anything you say."

Would likely be ignored. Still she had to say it.

"What about your car?" Dakota asked. "Have the cops located it?"

"No, but hopefully they will soon."

"Do you have a ride to your apartment?"

"Actually, it's a town house, near the hospital."

"Do you live alone?"

Her insides knotted. "No, Dakota. I don't live alone."

"I don't see a wedding band."

"I'm not married."

"Well, at least I can offer you a ride to the town house since you stayed extra hours with me."

"You don't have a vehicle here."

"Actually, I do. Another buddy dropped off my truck and Jim gave him a lift back to the hotel."

"You shouldn't be driving."

"The hotel's only a few miles away and the pain meds have pretty much worn off. I'm in good shape— Well, at least I'm clearheaded."

"You're in pain and should be keeping your right shoulder as still as possible."

He narrowed his gaze. "I'm left-handed." He sat up, yanking the hospital gown so that he stayed completely covered. "I promise to get you home safely."

Her physical safety was not the issue. She'd be in his truck. It would smell like him and feel like him. He'd be near enough for her to hear his breathing, and his presence would roll through her in heated swells.

"It's just a ride home, Viviana. I'm not promoting anything here."

"Okay, Dakota. Sure. I'd appreciate the ride."

Her heart was pounding as she left the room. But one thing was for certain. He would not be staying for breakfast this time.

DAKOTA TURNED THE KEY in the ignition, and his new Ford double cab pickup truck hummed to life. A George Strait tune blared from the radio and he reached over to lower the volume.

Viviana set a blue laptop case on the floor at her feet. "Nice wheels."

"Thanks."

"I thought you loved your old pickup."

"I did, but it had over a hundred thousand tough miles on it. It was ready to bite the dust."

She ran her hand over the dashboard. "I like this one."

"Yep. It has all the bells and whistles."

The silence grew awkward, punctuated by an awareness that all but consumed him. He'd been getting over her, or at least making a damn good stab at it. Now she was reviving the old feelings, torching the unhealed scars she'd left all over his heart.

He backed out of the parking spot. "Did the detective you called say whether or not there had been other armed carjackings in the area?"

"He said car thefts are on the rise, but that there hasn't been a carjacking in this area for a couple of years."

"Guess you never know when some thug will turn desperate."

"Apparently. Stay right when you leave the lot and then turn left at the light."

"Do you always work the late shift?" he asked once he'd made the turn.

"Normally I work from eleven at night to seven in the morning."

"Why was tonight different?"

"I was covering for a doctor friend who had tickets for a Michael Bublé concert."

"So she took your shift starting at eleven?"

"No. I'm starting a three-day break, so I wasn't on the schedule. E.R. hours run a little different from typical doctor's hours."

"Guess the graveyard shift is the bane of first-year staff doctors?"

"Not really. Having days off just suits my lifestyle better."

He understood what she meant. It gave her every evening at home with her significant other. The thought of her in another man's arms settled like lead in Dakota's stomach. Not that it surprised him. She'd never indicated she didn't want a man in her life—just not him.

"The next right," she said. "After that it's just a couple of blocks."

He did as she dictated, stopping in front of a two-story town house with a stone-and-wood fascia. A row of flowering shrubs set off a wide bay window. It was far more upscale than the small apartment she'd had as a resident back in Houston.

He wondered if she still had the same furniture. The couch where she'd given him the first massage to ease his painful muscles. His groin tightened as he remembered where that had led.

"Thanks for…"

"You need to take care of…"

They'd started talking at the exact same moment and their words became tangled.

She laughed nervously. "It was good to see you again, Dakota."

"Yeah. You, too." He leaned over, aching to kiss her, knowing it would be a big mistake.

She opened her door and slid out as if fearing he might make a move on her. He opened his truck door.

"Don't bother walking me to the door, Dakota. You're hurting, I'm exhausted and it really isn't necessary."

He watched her walk away, the finality of their brief encounter searing into his mind. She had her life all figured out and there was no place in it for him.

When she neared the house, motion lights flicked on. She looked back and waved. A few seconds later she turned the key in the lock and disappeared behind the dark wooden door.

He sat there for a few minutes, letting the memories wreak havoc with his brain before gunning the engine and starting off to his lonely hotel room.

He'd driven about four blocks when he stopped for a light and noticed Viviana's laptop case still on the floor. She might need the computer first thing in the morning, so there was nothing to do but take it back to her. Imagine her live-in's excitement to have an injured cowboy ring the bell in the wee hours of the morning.

There was movement in the shrubbery as he approached the house. He stopped and stared into the blackness. The movement evidently hadn't been enough to trigger the motion lights.

But something was in those bushes. He opened his truck door. A man jumped from behind the bushes and started running toward the back of the house. Dakota leaped from the truck and took off after him. With the first pounding of his feet on the pavement, pain shot through him like small explosions. He struggled for breath.

He got to the back of the house just in time to see the man jump from a branch, clearing the tall privacy fence and landing with a thud on the other side. By the time Dakota shinnied up the tree, the man had disappeared.

He dropped back to the ground, his breath knifing through his lungs. Damn. Had he not been thrown with such force tonight, he could have caught the man and taken him down. But if he hadn't wound up in the hospital, he wouldn't have run into Viviana. The gunman might have forced her into the car and abducted her. If this was the man who'd stolen her car, she was clearly not a random target.

He trudged back to the truck, retrieved the computer and took the walkway back to the front door in the faint glow of moonlight. The motion light had either quit working or more likely had been sabotaged. He looked and felt like hell as he rang the bell.

A minute later, Viviana opened the door a crack and peeked out at him. "What's wrong?"

"You left your computer in the truck. I brought it back to you."

She opened the door the rest of the way, then reached up and dislodged a leaf from his hair. "You're out of breath. Where have you been?"

"Chasing a man from your yard."

"What?"

"I spotted someone at your front window when I drove up. I chased him but he got away."

"The man who stole my car." Her voice was shaky.

"That would be my guess."

Color drained from her face. She took a deep breath and released it slowly. "I didn't mean to drag you into this."

"Best I remember, I came barging into it."

"So you did. Do you mind coming in while I call the cops?"

"What will your boyfriend say about that?"

"There is no boyfriend."

So her roommate was female or platonic. More relieved than he should be, Dakota stamped the dirt from his shoes and followed Viviana inside.

Viviana carefully locked the dead bolt behind Dakota. Twice tonight, he'd appeared just in time to save her from some depraved lunatic.

But right now, even that wasn't the worst of her problems. She'd known for seven months that she had to face Dakota again eventually. She'd tried to convince herself that she'd be able to look him in the eye and explain everything without her emotions billowing out of control.

But the second she'd heard his voice tonight, those illusions had vanished.

"You need to call the cops or your friendly detective right away," Dakota said. "The man could still be in the neighborhood and if they act fast they may be able to apprehend him."

"I will, but lower your voice and come with me to the kitchen."

"Why are we whispering?"

"Someone's asleep upstairs. There's an ice pack in the freezer." She opened a drawer, took out a dish towel and tossed it to him. "Wrap it in this and apply it to your shoulder."

"Bourbon would be better."

She opened the door to the cabinet where she kept her meager supply of liquor while she punched 911 into her cell phone. She was tempted to call Cortez again, but it was no use waking him in the middle of the night when there was little he could do at this point.

The 911 operator took her information.

"Are you certain you're not in any immediate danger?" the operator asked.

"I'm not certain, but the intruder appears to be gone."

"Stay on the line while I alert the police." The operator was back in under a minute. "An officer will be there within the next half hour. In the meantime, stay inside with your doors locked. If your situation changes and you feel you're in immediate danger, call 911 again."

"Did you stress to the police that this is likely the same man who stole my car earlier this evening?" Viviana asked.

"I made them aware of the circumstances."

"Thanks."

Which meant there was nothing to do but wait for the cops.

But at least that would give her a few minutes to clear her head and figure out how to handle Dakota.

Chapter Five

Pain was kicking in big-time. Dakota took a small bottle of aspirin from his shirt pocket and shook a few tablets into his hand.

"Meds and alcohol don't mix," Viviana cautioned.

"They do in my world." He downed them with the whiskey chaser. "Do you have a flashlight? I'd like to take a look at that bay window from the outside."

"You do realize it's almost three o'clock in the morning."

"I'd still like to check it out before a cop arrives."

"I was told to stay inside with the doors locked."

"And *you* should. So either hand me a flashlight or I'll get one out of my truck."

While Viviana opened a kitchen drawer

and rummaged for a flashlight, Dakota pulled a sharp knife from the rack at the back of the kitchen counter.

"There's really nothing the man could see from out there," Viviana explained as she handed him a shiny red flashlight. "The blinds were closed. And even from the front door, all you can see through the sidelights is the foyer."

"That's good to know."

"I'd rather you not go out there, Dakota. The man has a gun and he might come back."

"I hope he does, but it's not likely."

"What makes you think that?"

"He ran both times I showed up. He's not looking to use that gun if he doesn't have to. And he's not looking for a real fight."

"How do you know so much about criminals?"

"I watch *CSI* religiously."

Once outside, the steady whir of the air conditioner dominated the still, quiet air. Dakota squeezed through the shrubs so that he was pretty much in the same spot that the trespasser had been.

Just as Viviana had said, the blinds completely blocked any view of the inside of the house. That ruled out the guy just being a voyeur. So did the fact that the screen was missing.

Dakota sprayed a beam of light over the hedge. Sure enough, the screen was tucked into one of the bushes. He moved the beam back to the window. There were marks on the wood where the guy had tried to pry the window open.

No doubt about it, the guy had come back for her. Dakota's insides bucked at the thought of what might have happened if he hadn't showed up at that exact moment.

Viviana was waiting to open the door for him when he stepped in front of it.

"Do you have an alarm system?" Dakota asked.

"Yes, and it was set. It would have gone off instantly if the man had come through the door or the window."

"Nice in theory, but professional crooks disable them all the time. I'll check it."

"So much for feeling safe in my own house. Now that I think about it, the motion detector didn't come on when you went outside."

"I know. I suspect the bulb is crushed into the lawn behind the bushes."

Before Dakota could check the alarm system, the security company called on Viviana's cell phone to say they weren't getting a signal from the house phone line.

She assured them she was fine. They promised to send a technician out to check the system the following morning, though they suspected the problem was with the phone company.

Dakota suspected it was with a cut phone line.

"What if you hadn't come back tonight, Dakota? What then?" Viviana's voice shook. "That armed thug would be in my house right now."

Dakota slipped an arm around her shoulder. "I did come back. I'm here and I'm not going anywhere."

Viviana dropped to the sofa.

Seconds later, the flashing red lights of a squad car filtered through the sidelights for a few seconds before going dark. The sirens were silent.

Viviana raced to the front door. Dakota was only a step behind her, each hurried step a bitter reminder that physically, he was no match for anyone right now.

The two uniformed police officers showed their IDs and once they'd taken seats in the cozy living room, they got down to business. Dakota let Viviana do most of the talking, though he did have to explain that he didn't get a good look at the guy he'd chased off.

Nothing in the questioning jumped out at Dakota until the younger of the cops, a guy named Greg Simmons, started asking more pointed questions.

"Is there anyone who might have a reason to target you, Dr. Mancini?"

Viviana fingered the small gold heart that dangled from a chain around her neck. "Yes, I talked to Detective Cortez earlier tonight. I'm sure he'll follow up on that first thing in the morning, but—"

The cop interrupted. "Harry Cortez, in homicide?"

She nodded.

"How did you come to talk to him?"

"I know him from a case he's investigating."

The older cop leaned forward. "What case would that be?"

"The Compton case. I admitted Leslie Compton to the hospital the night she died of abuse. The case goes to trial in nine days. I'm one of the prosecutor's witnesses."

The cop nodded as if that explained a lot. "So you're involved in the case against Hank Bateman."

"Yes, but it wasn't Hank Bateman who stole my car. I would have recognized him. if you need to know more, I suggest you talk to Detective Cortez."

"We'll make sure he sees this report."

"I've told you everything. Wouldn't it be more useful now for you to be searching the neighborhood for the man who tried to break in my house—whoever he may be?"

"Yes, ma'am. We'll get on that. Keep your doors locked and if there's any more trouble, call 911 again. I'll see that someone's in the neighborhood for the rest of the night."

"I appreciate that."

Dakota stood and tried to wrap his mind around the new fragments of information. Viviana was to be a witness in a case against a man the cops seemed to know well. That was never a good sign.

She was massaging her right temple when she rejoined him after seeing the officers to the door. She dropped to the sofa. "We need to talk."

Her tone indicated this wouldn't be pleasant. "About the Compton case?"

"No, that's far too detailed to go into tonight. We need to talk about *us*."

As if that would be easy. "Whatever you need to say about us has waited sixteen months. Another eight hours can't hurt. So if it's all the same with you, I say we crash."

"You can't stay here. I don't even have an extra bed."

He patted the sofa cushion. "This works fine. And don't worry, I'm a light sleeper. I'll wake at the first sign of trouble. Not that I expect there to be any more tonight."

"You don't have to stay."

"I'm staying."

"Then I guess we should just crash."

She didn't sound excited about having him as an overnight guest, but she did sound relieved. He wasn't sure if it was because he was sticking around for protection or because she could put off the conversation she was obviously dreading.

She walked away but returned a few minutes later with sheets, a pillow and a fresh ice pack. The moment grew uncomfortable. Saying a friendly good-night to a woman with whom he'd shared the hottest sex of his life, albeit months before, was downright prickly.

They managed it. He watched her walk up the stairs, the gentle sway of her hips as seductive as ever.

A few hours ago, he'd had nothing on his mind but riding a bull. Now he was consumed with Viviana, and everything had become complex and tangled.

Worse, he had a feeling deep in his gut that the complications were going to get a lot worse before this was over.

DAKOTA'S FEET stretched over the end of the sofa, making it impossible to get into a comfortable position. A nagging headache sat at the back of his skull. Breathing hurt. His muscles ached.

Unable to sleep, his mind juggled the night's events. It was purely coincidence that he'd arrived on the scene at the exact moment that Viviana was being attacked.

But how much of the rest of what happened was coincidence? Random attack or targeted?

A determined bastard coming to finish what he'd started at the hospital?

And if Viviana had been targeted, was Hank Bateman behind it? Dakota would need to know a lot more about the Compton case before he could even make an intelligent guess.

He could call his brother Wyatt. Consulting a good homicide detective made sense, and Wyatt was one of the best. But calling him in Atlanta would open a whole new set of thorny dilemmas.

Two of Dakota's brothers lived in or near their hometown of Mustang Run. Dylan lived on Willow Creek Ranch with their father; Sean lived close by in Bandera. His brother Tyler planned to move back to the ranch as soon as he finished his stint in the army. His wife, Julie, was already there.

Dylan, Tyler and Sean had let go of the past and embraced Troy Ledger as if he were Santa Claus coming down the chimney on Christmas Eve. It worked for them.

Dakota wanted no part of it. At this late date, he wasn't about to start wallowing in the mud while pretending it was chocolate.

Dakota stretched and cringed as he sucked

in the pain. He hadn't hurt this bad since…
since he'd been kicked by a bull the night he'd
first met Viviana. Or maybe since the night
they'd said goodbye and he'd rode off into the
sunset in his then-aging pickup truck.

There were all kinds of hurtin'.

He'd get over the pain in his muscles and
joints soon enough, but he might as well face
facts. Even if Viviana told him his presence
around here wasn't wanted or needed, which
he figured was the basis for the promised dis-
cussion, he'd be in no shape to ride or rack up
points for the next few nights.

VIVIANA JERKED AWAKE to the sound of foot-
falls on the stairs. She glanced at the clock—
7:00 a.m. No doubt Claire was going to the
kitchen to start a pot of coffee, just as she
did most mornings about this time. Only normally Viviana would be just finishing up her
graveyard shift.

This morning when Claire went for the
morning newspaper, she'd spy the hunky
cowboy on the sofa. The officious nanny
would not consider that a pleasant surprise.

Viviana untangled her feet from the sheets,
jumped from the bed and grabbed her ivory-

colored silk robe. She'd have to get downstairs on the double to explain—or run interference—since somehow Claire had slept right through last night's drama. As had Briana.

The sixty-something nanny was in super physical condition, but she did have a slight hearing problem. She didn't wear her aids when she slept, but she kept the baby monitor on the bedside table near her ear so that she'd hear Briana's slightest whimper.

Poking her arms through the sleeves of the robe, Viviana made a quick stop at the door to the nursery. Briana stirred and stretched her pudgy little arms over her head when the door squeaked open, but thankfully her eyes remained closed.

The smell of coffee drifted up the staircase. Dakota must have beat Claire to the brew task. Impulsively, Viviana smoothed her hair and pulled the robe tighter, looping the belt to keep the robe closed.

Her pulse quickened as she pictured Dakota in her kitchen making coffee. Barefoot. His hair rumpled. Wearing his briefs…or nothing at all. The memories of how it had once been spilled into her mind and Viviana trembled as heat suffused her body.

She paused when she reached the bottom step, and her fingers wrapped tightly around the newel cap as she eavesdropped on the conversation.

"Now who did you say you are again?"

"Dakota Ledger."

"And you're an old friend of Viviana's?"

"That's right."

Viviana hurried to the kitchen before Dakota had to answer any more questions, and before he started asking any. He was barefoot and shirtless, but fortunately wearing jeans.

"I see you two have met," Viviana said.

"Yes, and he's lucky I didn't ram a knife through him. I sure didn't expect to find a strange man in the kitchen."

"Sorry I didn't warn you," Viviana said, "but his visit was unexpected. I ran into him in the E.R. and, well, he just wasn't in any shape to go home alone. I thought he should stay here in case his pain became worse during the night."

She did not want to explain the ordeal of last night to Claire. If she tried, Claire would ask a million questions and give at least an hour's worth of advice.

Claire studied the bruises on Dakota's chest and shoulder. "Were you in an accident?"

"You could say that. I got thrown from a bull."

"Seriously?"

"Serious as a kick to the ribs."

"Hmmph."

Her skeptical tone no doubt summed up not only Claire Evers's feelings on bull riding, but also her thoughts on his having spent the night.

Viviana pulled some mugs from the cabinet over the coffeemaker. "Thanks for filling in for me last night, Claire."

"You know I don't mind staying when you need me."

"And I really appreciate that. I won't need you anymore today and you probably have things you need to do." It was the most tactful way she could think of to get rid of Claire.

"I don't have anything planned. I can stay if you need me."

"No. I can handle things."

"In that case, I'll just get my handbag and head out. I'll be back on Wednesday evening at my regular time."

"Are you the housekeeper?" Dakota asked.

"Lands, no. I'm the nanny. I've taken care of Briana since six weeks after she was born. Viviana says she doesn't trust anyone but me with her baby."

"Viviana's baby?" Dakota leaned against the counter, so stunned the words were a husky whisper.

"Yes. The doctor's daughter. Briana? Who did you think I was talking about?"

"Just checking." He stood perfectly still, staring at Viviana without saying a word until Claire was out of hearing range. "You never mentioned having a baby," he said accusingly.

"You didn't ask." She poured two mugs of coffee and handed one to him. "I guess you still take it black."

"Forget the coffee. How old is the baby?"

"Seven months."

"Seven months. Does that mean you were pregnant with another man's child when we were together?"

This was not the way Viviana had planned this encounter. Only, that was the real problem. She'd never been able to visualize exactly what she'd say or how Dakota would react. And she was starting to resent his attitude.

"I don't remember you asking or caring if I was in another relationship at the time. But I wasn't pregnant when we met, Dakota. I was pregnant when you left."

"You're not saying…"

"Yes, I'm saying you have a precious, adorable daughter—Briana. You don't have to take my word for it. You can swab her cheek and have a paternity test if that would make you feel better. But I wasn't with another man for months before I met you and I haven't been with one since."

Briana began to wail. She was a terrific baby, but she had a horrific sense of timing.

Viviana left Dakota standing in the kitchen staring into space like a zombie while she climbed the steps to the nursery to get Briana from her crib. It was past time the little darling met her bruised and battered cowboy daddy.

Chapter Six

Dakota reeled from the shocking announcement. There had to be a mistake. This could not be happening to him. He had no idea how to be a father. How could he? He'd certainly never had a role model to follow.

Questions and denials stormed his mind as Viviana stepped into the kitchen balancing a smiling kid on her hip. He turned away as if that would make the whole ordeal disappear.

Viviana stopped a few feet from him. "This is Briana. Look at her, Dakota. She has your eyes, and your smile."

He turned slowly and his heart felt as if it were twisting inside him.

The child looked at him sheepishly from beneath dark lashes. "Gob a ga ga."

His insides churned. His kid, but he didn't see himself in her. He saw Viviana. Dark hair that curled close to her scalp. Cute nose, with the slightest of upturn. Rosy cheeks. But...

"She's so little."

"Not really," Viviana said. "Her growth curve is well within the average range. She's healthy and normal."

Viviana held the child out for him to take. He backed away.

"You don't have to be afraid of her, Dakota. She won't bite, though she is cutting a tooth."

"She's getting a tooth?" He sounded like a parrot, but who knew babies got teeth so soon?

"Have you ever been around babies?"

"Not that I remember." He sank to the sofa. "Why didn't you tell me I was a father before this?"

"Exactly how was I supposed to do that? Send a post card in care of a bull somewhere between the two coasts?"

"I have a cell phone."

"With a new, *unlisted* number."

He mumbled a curse under his breath. He'd changed his server and his number when some emotionally unstable buckle bunny had started calling him all hours of the day and night. Only...

"I didn't change that number until three months after I was with you."

"That's how long it took before I realized I was pregnant. I was doing my residency in emergency medicine, remember? I was working so many hours that when I was home I simply collapsed into bed. Days turned into weeks before I realized how long it had been since I'd had a period."

He did remember her long hours at the hospital. She'd been about to start a rare four-day break when he'd first met her. They'd spent every second of that time together. Then she'd gone back to her residency and worked from sunup to midnight. She'd come home exhausted. But even those two nights, she'd fallen hungrily into his arms.

And then he'd had to leave in time to make the next big bull-riding event. She'd decided that it should be a permanent goodbye. Their lives were too different. They would never make it as a couple.

He couldn't argue that. He'd never thought of himself as husband material. He was too much of a realist for that. But that didn't mean he was ready to just toss away what they had.

And now they had a daughter. The idea of it scared him to death.

"It's not as if I didn't try to reach you, Dakota, but you have no permanent address. If you do, I don't have it."

"I didn't exactly fall off the face of the earth. You could have contacted the Professional Bull Riders Association. They could have gotten word to me."

"I didn't even know there was an association, and frankly, by the time I'd tried everything else, I wasn't sure it was worth the effort."

"What is that supposed to mean?"

Briana began to squirm in her arms. Viviana pulled a padded quilt square from a basket by the sofa and spread it on the floor with one hand while she balanced the baby on her hip. She lay Briana on the quilt, then dug out a colorful rattling ball and a set of large plastic keys from the same basket and placed them on the quilt beside her.

Briana rolled over and pulled up to her hands and knees as if she were going to crawl away. Instead she started rocking back and forth and making gurgling noises.

Dakota was mesmerized by her movements, the sounds she made, her short pudgy arms and legs, the funny way she stuck her behind in the air. Yet he kept his distance.

"It means exactly what's happening right now," Viviana said, as if the conversation hadn't been interrupted. "You're afraid to interact with Briana at all. Getting to know her might interfere with your life, might make you reconsider your priorities. And we both know you live for the competition."

"The way you live for your medical career."

That was a knee-jerk statement and totally unfair. Viviana was obviously devoted to Briana. But Viviana's comments were just as unmerited. She'd had months to mentally prepare to be a mother. He'd had a matter of minutes to adjust to being a dad.

Not that he was sure more time would have made a difference. He knew his limitations. He had nothing to offer as a father except bad genes and a killer reputation.

"What's Briana's full name?"

"Briana Marie Ledger. Marie is for my mother."

And Ledger was a curse.

"I don't need anything from you, Dakota, if that's what you're worried about. I can raise Briana on my own and I'd rather do that unless you truly want to be in her life. I won't see her hurt and rejected by a man who's a father in name only."

It wasn't a matter of wanting to be a part of Briana's life. It was that the only thing he had to offer was money. Fortunately, winning the world title two years ago assured he had plenty. "I'll support her financially. She'll never do without anything she needs. "

Viviana winced as if he'd slapped her. "Don't bother, Dakota. *I* can give her everything she needs—except you."

Viviana picked up Briana and hugged her tight. "I'll be upstairs for the rest of the morning. Just let me know when you leave so that I can lock the door behind you."

"I won't be leaving anytime soon. I have locks to change. You need something stronger and more secure than what you have now."

"I can call a locksmith."

Shock, frustration and the fact that his arm hurt every time he moved it were eating away at his patience. "Will it kill you to just let me change the locks?"

"Suit yourself."

Viviana turned and walked away, leaving

him to struggle with the fact that his life had just changed forever.

DAKOTA WAS SO SORE he could barely move, but he couldn't sit still, either. And thinking about his new status as a father struck him with the kind of fear that would paralyze him if he let it.

He didn't want to leave Viviana and Briana alone until he was certain they were safe. Yet he did want to get started on those locks.

His cell phone rang. The caller ID said Jim Angle. One problem solved. He took the call.

"Morning, Jim. You're just the man I need to talk to."

"I guess you want me to come rescue you from a wicked nurse?"

"No, I'm out of the hospital."

"Ready to take on a bull?"

"That's doubtful for tonight."

"So how are you?"

"I'm a little beat-up," Dakota admitted, "but I'm making it. Nothing's broken."

"That's good news. I'll drop by your hotel room and bring you some breakfast."

"I'm not at the hotel."

"So where the hell are you?"

"I spent the night at Viviana Mancini's house, or at least what was left of the night after the hospital finally released me."

"Well, ain't you just riding the gravy train with biscuit wheels? Does that mean you're back in the saddle?"

"Far from it. It's a long story. I'll fill you in later, but right now I could use a favor."

"You got it, as long as I can still get back to the arena for tonight's show."

"That I can guarantee."

Dakota explained what he needed in the way of tools and locks from the hardware store. An hour later Jim arrived with everything on the list and some spares. Two hours later, they were done, thanks to the fact that Jim did not move with the ineptness of a guy with a bum shoulder and bruised ribs.

A few minutes after Jim left, a troubleshooter from the security company arrived to repair the system. The technician reiterated what Dakota already knew. The system had been disarmed by someone who knew exactly what he was doing.

Viviana ventured downstairs without Briana while the tech guy was there. When he left, she disappeared into her upstairs inner sanctum again.

Dakota's efforts to keep her safe were apparently not winning him any points. Not that he was expecting any, but the tension between them was getting to him.

Dakota had about decided he should just go back to the hotel and depend on the locks to keep her safe when the doorbell rang again. Before Dakota could see who'd come calling, Viviana came running down the stairs, again without Briana.

"It's Detective Cortez," she said.

"How do you know?"

"He just called on my cell phone to say he was dropping by to talk about last night." She opened the door and ushered in a man who'd never grace the cover of *GQ*.

Cortez looked to be in his late forties and was slightly overweight. His chin was dotted with yesterday's whiskers and a smear of what looked like blackberry jelly decorated the front of a wrinkled blue sport shirt.

Perspiration beaded on the detective's forehead. He pulled a handkerchief from his back pocket and dabbed at the moisture.

"I heard you made a call to 911 last night," Cortez offered, in lieu of a proper greeting.

"That goon who stole my car tried to break into my house," Viviana said.

"Did you see him?"

"No, but Dakota did."

Cortez turned toward Dakota as if just realizing he was in the room. "Are you Dakota?"

"I am."

Cortez reached into pocket and pulled out a piece of paper. He unfolded it and handed it to Dakota. A black-and-white mug shot stared back at him.

"Is this the man you saw?"

"Is that Hank Bateman?"

"Not the best picture of him, but yeah, that's him. Do you recognize this man?"

"No. He doesn't look familiar and I'm sure I would have remembered that ghastly tattoo on his neck."

"Can you describe the man you saw outside the town house?"

"No. It was dark and he was mostly hidden by the shrubs that border the bay window. He ran when I drove up. I chased him, but he got away."

"Did he fire at you?"

"Thankfully, no."

"Did you see a weapon?"

"No, but I was never all that close to him."

"Won't you sit down, Detective?" Viviana urged. "When you finish I have quite a few questions of my own."

"I figured you might." He took a seat in the overstuffed chair across from the sofa.

"Can I get you some coffee?" Viviana asked.

"Already too hot for coffee. And it's not even July yet. I could use a glass of ice water, though."

"I'll be right back."

Detective Cortez crossed an ankle over the opposite knee. "You got a last name, Dakota, or is Dakota even your real first name?"

"The name's Dakota Ledger, and I don't have any reason to lie about it."

"Ledger." Cortez's mouth screwed into a frown. "I thought you looked familiar when I came in. You're that bull rider in town for the competition. I saw your picture in the newspaper yesterday."

"That would be me."

"Dakota Ledger."

He said the name again, this time as if it left a foul taste in his mouth.

"I hear your famous father's back in Mustang Run now."

"That wasn't in the newspaper."

"No, but I'm a curious man. The name rang a bell when I read about you so I looked you up. You were what…six at the time your mother was murdered?"

"Something like that."

"How do you know Dr. Mancini?"

Clearly none of the man's business. "Am I under investigation?"

"Not that I'm aware of—at least not yet."

Viviana rejoined them with the water.

The detective gulped about half of it down. "Why don't you tell me exactly what happened last night, Dr. Mancini, and then I'll see if I can answer your questions."

She started to introduce Dakota. The detective informed her they'd already met. She went through everything again without one interruption from Cortez. Dakota figured he'd already read it all in last night's police report anyway.

"You said Hank Bateman might up the

ante," Viviana said. "Showing up with a gun would certainly qualify."

"I don't put anything past him. I'm just surprised he'd let someone else do his dirty work now that he's out on bail. I'm even more surprised that he didn't make it clear that he was there to convince you not to testify. Hank is not one to beat around the bush."

"But you do think he was behind the car theft and attempted break-in?"

"It's not all adding up, but I'll find out if he's behind this. Count on that."

"I am. I have to."

The detective put both feet on the floor and leaned forward in his chair.

"Shouldn't you be getting ready to ride a bull, Ledger?"

"I'm giving the bull a break tonight."

The detective's brows arched, but he didn't comment on the statement. Instead, he turned back to Viviana.

"I've got a lineup scheduled this afternoon for a man whose convenience-store customers have been robbed three times in the last four weeks. It's the usual suspects for his area. I'd like for you to come down and see if you recognize any of the suspects A couple of them run with Bateman's old gang, so he might have hired one of them to put the fear into you."

"I just gave the nanny the day off, but I'll try to get a babysitter for Briana. Just tell me what time and where."

"They should be ready for you about two-thirty at the precinct. Here's the address." He pulled a business card from his pocket and set it next to the water. "In the meantime, keep your doors locked, and let me know if you hear from Hank. I'd love a reason to force the judge to put him behind bars again."

Cortez finished his water and stood to leave.

Dakota stood as well, the movement sending a few sharp spikes of pain along his chest wall. He had a few questions of his own.

"If a guy can handily disable an alarm system, don't you think he could hot-wire a car?"

Cortez scratched his chin. "What's your point?"

"The guy was waiting in the parking lot last night with a loaded gun. Seems unnecessary unless it was more than the car he wanted."

"Say what's on your mind, Dakota."

"The intent might have been to abduct Viviana. That would have given the gunman or even Hank the time and opportunity to frighten Viviana into refusing to testify."

"Tell you what, Ledger. You leave the detective work to me. I'll leave the bull riding to you."

"That's okay," Dakota said. "You feel free to ride a bull if you want. You could also put a tail on Hank Bateman 24/7. Then you'd know exactly what he's up to and he might lead you to the guy who took Viviana's car."

Cortez smirked and walked to the door.

Viviana walked with him. "This isn't related," she said, "but do you have an ID on the gunshot victim who died in the E.R. last night?"

"We do. His name was Kevin Lucas."

"Was he married?"

"Divorced. Thankfully, with no kids."

"Do you know who shot him?"

"No suspects yet. And no motive."

"I think he was trying to tell me something just before he died," Viviana said.

"You didn't mention that last night."

"I forgot in the chaos, and I doubt it's anything you can use. His words were garbled, and all he got out was something that sounded like *Shell*. I think he was trying to say more."

"He could have been referring to anything. But don't worry, I'll get the guy who did it, just like I'll find out who accosted you and stole your car. It just takes time."

Dakota liked that kind of confidence as long as the detective lived up to his own hype. If the detective didn't keep Bateman away from Viviana, Dakota would, even if he had to fight her to do it.

Once the detective left, Viviana walked into the kitchen. Dakota followed her. "I need to go to my hotel and get cleaned up," he said, talking to the back of her head.

"Do what you like."

"I don't want you and Briana staying here alone. You'll have to go with me."

Viviana spun around. "You're not the one making the decisions, Dakota."

Dakota's muscles flexed. He crossed the room and tugged her around to face him.

"Let go of me."

"Not until you listen to what I have to say."

"No, Dakota. You listen to me. Our only tie is Briana and you've pretty much said you want nothing to do with her."

"I never said that. She's my daughter. You're her mother. I have a stake in keeping you both safe and I intend to do just that. But right now I have to take a shower and put on some clean clothes before I start to look like Dirty Harry."

He relaxed his hold on her, but she didn't move away.

"You will never look like Cortez."

It was the first time he'd seen her smile in sixteen months. His heart melted like an ice cube in the hot Texas sun. There was no getting over Viviana.

DAKOTA'S HOTEL WAS MORE luxurious than Viviana had anticipated, yet the room smelled of leather, a woodsy aftershave and pure masculinity. A large, open duffel rested on the luggage rack, revealing a stack of freshly laundered Western shirts and neatly folded jeans.

She paced the spacious room, trying to ignore the ambiance and the sound of running water. To think of Dakota in the shower meant visualizing his beautiful, hard body, naked and wet. She'd never showered with a lover before she'd met Dakota. Never realized the thrill of having every inch of her hot, slick body caressed by warm, tantalizing hands.

Her pulse skyrocketed as the erotic memories took hold. For six days last year, she'd forgotten rules and inhibitions and given in to every desire Dakota had inspired. They'd picnicked naked in bed, had sex in every room of her small apartment, even the hallway. They'd snuggled in front of the fire, ruined her best set of sheets with drizzled chocolate, laughed at nothing, smiled because they simply couldn't stop.

The week had been a fantasy; she'd experienced nonstop fireworks and emotional highs that had made her as giddy as a teenager. The one thing they hadn't done was talk. She didn't know him. He knew even less about her. What she did know spelled disaster.

He thrived on excitement. She craved stability.

He lived out of his suitcase in hotel rooms, waking up in a new town every week for most of the year. He never spent too many nights in the same town. She required continuity and routine, the same town, the same house, the same bed. No risks.

The bathroom door opened and Dakota

stepped out, chasing away her memories. His hair was wet and dripping onto his bare shoulders. A fluffy white towel was looped just below his waist. His bare feet were almost soundless on the thick carpet as he walked toward her, smelling of soap and looking good enough to eat.

She turned away while he retrieved his clothes from the duffel.

"No need to be embarrassed, Viviana. You've seen it all before."

"That was different."

"Right. Then you weren't acting like I had the plague."

"I'm not trying to avoid you. It's just…"

"Just what, Viviana? Because to tell you the truth, I haven't really changed all that much in sixteen months. I was just a bull-riding cowboy even then."

Her phone rang and she took the call, thankful to escape the conversation that had nowhere to go except in the tank. "Hello."

"Is this Dr. Mancini?"

"Yes. To whom am I speaking?"

"This is Melody Hollister with the D.A.'s office. I'm Nick Jefferson's assistant. We've spoken several times before in regard to the Compton case, but it's been a while."

"Yes, I remember. Please don't tell me the trial has been postponed again. I really need to get this over with."

"No, everything is set to go as scheduled one week from tomorrow. We will have a different judge presiding, however."

"Detective Cortez informed me of the change. Will it be a problem?"

"I don't anticipate anything interfering with a conviction of homicide. All we have to do is prove that Hank Bateman knew that his actions would likely result in death for Leslie Compton."

"How could he not know that shaking her senseless could be fatal? She was an infant."

"Exactly. We have a psychiatrist who will testify to his mental and emotional state. Mr. Jefferson's questions to you will basically focus on the medical condition of the child. If the defense attorney's questions stray beyond what you testified in your deposition, Mr. Jefferson will object."

"Okay."

"There is one concern."

Viviana's hand tightened on the phone. "Does it involve Hank Bateman?"

"No. It involves Karen Compton, the dead infant's mother."

Frustration hit hard. "Hank got to her, didn't he? She's decided not to testify."

"Not that we're aware of, but we're currently unable to locate her. She hasn't shown up for work in over a week and no one in her family has seen or heard from her."

"Do you think Hank's behind the disappearance?"

"It's possible," Melody said, "but unfortunately, she has a history of vanishing like this, sometimes for weeks at a time. Then when the man she's run off with stops buying her drugs, she comes home, or so say her neighbors."

"And this was the mother of that precious baby who was literally shaken to death," Viviana said. "So sad."

"Yes, and I wish it was the first case like this I've seen, but these things happen far too often in the current drug culture."

Viviana couldn't help but think of Briana. So helpless. So dependent. So precious. She was glad she'd dropped her off at Claire's this afternoon instead of having Claire come to the town house. Though she hated to admit it to Dakota, she was nervous about being in her own house unless he was there with them.

"I'll testify," she said. "Count on it. Leslie Compton was completely vulnerable and innocent. She had a right to love and life."

By the time the call was over, Dakota was dressed and ready to go, looking so like the charismatic cowboy man she'd fallen for that her heart did a nosedive.

"Bad news?" he asked.

"I'll tell you about it in the car on the way to the police precinct."

"In that case, let's get out of here." He fit a shaving kit into the duffel before zipping it and slinging the strap over his shoulder. Then he grabbed what looked like a bag of dirty clothes.

Her breath caught. "Are you moving out of the hotel?"

"For the time being. It would be a little crowded and inconvenient for you and Briana to stay here until after the trial so that means you'll have to put up with me at your place."

"The trial is not for another eight days. What about your competition?"

"It can wait." He put a hand to the small of her back and urged her toward the door. His touch was unassuming, seductive. Protective.

And here she went again. Falling hard and setting herself up for a broken heart. Would she never learn?

Chapter Seven

"You told me Dr. Mancini didn't have a boy-friend."

"She didn't. I swear. I watched her come and go from her house for a week. She was always alone. For the most part she just went to work and back home. And then all of a sudden this cowboy shows up."

"You let a friggin' cowboy interfere with the plan. What part of doing whatever it takes did you not get?"

"I get it. There's just been a slight delay, but I'll take care of it. You can count on me."

"Obviously, I can't."

"Don't talk like that. We're a team."

"I guess we'll see about that in time, won't we? And time is running out."

Chapter Eight

Troy Ledger rinsed the lone plate under the kitchen faucet as he chewed and swallowed the last bite of his ham sandwich. It was two in the afternoon, but he'd missed lunch. He'd been hard at work since before dawn, fixing the roof on his storage barn. It was only late June, but the heat index had climbed to the mid-nineties today.

He took his glass of iced tea and walked into the family room, slowing as he passed the hearth. Without warning the familiar feeling that he was being sucked into a vacuum attacked with a near paralyzing force.

For the first few weeks after his release from prison, he had felt that way every time he walked into this room. The room where Helene had been murdered. Shot twice in the head, once in the chest. All three bullets fired at close range.

He'd found her like that, blood matted in her beautiful black hair, her eyes empty and vacant, her skin already cool to the touch. He was late coming in for lunch that day, too. If he hadn't have been, she might still be alive.

The dark memories crept from the haunted crevices of his mind and he stopped and leaned against the back of his recliner until he could steady himself.

He'd been out of prison for a year now, and he was no closer to finding Helene's killer. The beast who'd stolen his wife and the mother of his five sons was still a free man… unless he'd gone to jail for another crime. That possibility offered little consolation.

The house was an empty shell without her yet there were nights the walls seemed to vibrate with her presence. He could hear the echo of her laughter or her sweet voice singing one of the boys a lullaby. Those were the nights his arms ached to hold her and his mind conjured up images that made ragged shreds of his heart.

A weight settled on Troy's shoulders and he walked to the bookcase and studied the framed photos that his neighbor Ruthanne referred to as Helene's shrine. It wasn't. It was a tribute to the person she'd been.

He picked up the picture of Helene standing in the front yard holding Dakota in her arms. He was no more than a few months old at the time.

When she'd first realized she was pregnant, Helene had talked of nothing but how she hoped number five would be a girl. And then when she was five months along, she'd started to bleed. They'd rushed her to the hospital but it was touch-and-go for a few days as to whether she'd miscarry.

After that, all she cared about was that the baby growing inside her would be born healthy. Dakota filled that bill to perfection. He was smaller than the other four had been, but healthy and content, almost never crying. Helene had called him her miracle child, her last baby. She'd cried for hours the day he'd started kindergarten.

Still holding the picture, Troy walked to the master bedroom and then through the sliding glass doors to the courtyard garden. Helene's garden, though it was his daughter-in-law Collette who kept it in shape now.

He dropped to the ornate metal bench and watched the honeybees dart among the blossoms and the two hummingbirds that were dive-bombing each other over territorial rights to the sugar water in their feeder. He sat the picture on the seat beside him, leaned back and closed his eyes.

I let you down, Helene. I let you down in so many ways. I didn't fight hard enough to stay out of prison. I was consumed with grief and naive enough that I believed innocent until proven guilty was more than an empty premise.

I wasn't here for the boys. Dakota's stubborn, like I am. I don't know if he'll ever come home and give me a chance to prove I'm not the monster he's convinced I am.

"I thought I might find you out here."

He jumped at the voice, then turned to the glass door he'd left open behind him. "Ruthanne, have you ever heard of ringing the doorbell?"

"I rang it. You didn't answer. But your truck was parked in front so I figured you might be out here."

She joined him in the garden, her high heels clacking against the rough stone walkway. Her straight black skirt was a snug fit on her shapely body and the emerald green of her blouse set off her fiery eyes. She was damned attractive for a woman her age. Too bad she was so annoying.

She took the garden chair and crossed her legs so that the skirt rode up to indecent levels. "You know it's time you stop just sitting around grieving for a woman who's been dead for nineteen years."

"I don't just sit around. I work a ranch."

"You should get out more. The Stevensons are having a cocktail fundraiser next weekend for their son-in-law who's running for agriculture commissioner. You should go."

"I wasn't invited."

"You could go as my guest."

"I'm busy."

"Doing what?"

"I don't know yet."

"You are one hardheaded man, Troy Ledger. Anyway, I didn't just stop by to point out your faults. I came to ask if you'd read the Austin paper this morning."

"No, should I have?"

"There was a brief mention of Dakota in one of the columns in the spotlight section."

He set up straighter, his interest piqued. "What did it say about him?"

"Apparently there's a bull-riding event in San Antonio this week and many of the country's top bull riders are participating. Dakota was one of the ones they named."

In San Antonio and Dakota hadn't even bothered to call, much less come for a visit. Troy tried to hide the hurt from Ruthanne. "What did they say about him?"

"That he was the world champion two years ago."

"I already knew that. My grandson Joey and I caught him on cable TV a few months ago. We've managed to see him several times since."

"He was injured last night. The paper said he was thrown and the bull kicked him in the chest."

Troy got a sick feeling in the pit of his stomach. "Did they say how serious the injuries were?"

"Only that they were bad enough to send him to the emergency room. At the time the article was written, they weren't sure if he'd be able to participate tonight. I thought you'd want to call and check on him if you hadn't already heard from him."

"I hadn't heard." Troy hated to admit that he didn't even know how to get in touch with his youngest son.

Maybe Wyatt could track him down. Or it could be that Dylan or Sean had Dakota's phone number.

Troy wondered what Dakota would say if he just showed up at his hotel room.

"I have the newspaper in the car if you want it," Ruthanne said.

"I'd appreciate that."

"There's also an interesting article on my ex."

"Dare I ask what our illustrious senator is up to now?"

"Another senator filed for divorce and claimed irreconcilable differences. He says his wife is having an affair with Riley."

"Another juicy scandal to entertain those inside the beltway."

"Riley was always good at providing that. Neither he nor your friend Able Drake ever knew when to keep their pants zipped."

"You can't compare Able to Riley."

"Of course I can. You never could see what

was going on right under your eyes, but I wasn't that blind."

"What's that supposed to mean?"

"You figure it out." She stepped closer, reached over and let a painted fingernail trail his jawbone. "Let me know what you discover about Dakota. And in the meantime, if you find yourself in need of feminine company, you know where to find me."

"I'll keep that in mind."

He walked to the car with Ruthanne to get the newspaper. If Dakota was seriously hurt, Troy would find a way to see him. Whether Dakota liked the fact or not, he was Troy's son.

"THAT WAS A COMPLETE WASTE of time," Viviana said as they left the police station. "At least it was for me. Hopefully the convenience-shop owner had better luck."

"It's too bad they haven't found your car. It could have usable fingerprints."

"I'm just glad I didn't get in that car with the thug."

Dakota opened the passenger door of his truck and waited while she climbed in. "I'm famished," he said. "How about a late lunch?"

"I'm not sure I can eat. My stomach has been tied in knots ever since I saw that gun last night. I'll sit with you while you eat."

But first she wanted to call and check on Briana. Not that her daughter wasn't perfectly safe and in good hands with Claire.

Viviana's cell phone rang before she got the chance to make the call. This time she checked the caller ID, but to no avail. It said *Unavailable.* "Hopefully, it's news that they've found my car." She flipped it open.

"Hello."

"Is this Dr. Mancini?" The caller was female and her voice was low and shaky.

"Yes, but I'm not on duty. If you're having an emergency, you should call 911."

"It's not an emergency, at least not that kind of emergency. But I need to talk to you. It's important."

"Who is this?"

"Shelby Lucas. You don't know me, but you were my brother's physician last night."

"You're Kevin Lucas's sister?"

"Yes, ma'am."

That explained his last muddled murmurings. He was trying to give her a message for his sister. "I'm sorry I was unable to do more for him, but there was no way to save him."

"I know. That's what the police detective said."

"If you need any information from Kevin's medical file with the E.R., you'll need to check with hospital records."

"Thanks, but I really need to talk to you in person. Can we meet somewhere?"

"I'm not at the hospital today and there's really nothing I can say except that the bullets entered the skull and did extensive damage to the brain tissue."

"I didn't call about Kevin."

"Then I don't understand."

"I called about Hank Bateman." Her voice dropped so low that Viviana couldn't be sure she'd heard her right.

"Did you say Hank Bateman?"

"Yes."

Viviana felt Dakota's gaze boring into her as he turned into the parking lot of a chain steakhouse.

"How do you know Hank?"

"I'll explain, just not over the phone. I can call you back. I have to go now."

"Wait. We're stopping for lunch. You can meet us at the restaurant."

"I need to talk in private."

"That's not possible, but anything you have to say you can say in front of my friend. He knows about the trial and my dealings with Bateman. You can trust him as much as you trust me."

"Which restaurant?" Shelby's voice had dropped to a whisper, as if she were afraid someone would overhear her conversation.

Viviana gave her the name and the address and described the sapphire-blue blouse and the white capris she was wearing.

She heard a man's booming voice and then a click as Shelby broke the connection. She had a growing suspicion that Shelby Lucas would not keep their rendezvous.

She went back and saved the number Shelby had called from. Any information about Hank Bateman might come in handy before the trial was over.

It was midafternoon and the restaurant was quiet. Viviana tried to remember what Dakota liked to eat, but she wasn't sure they'd had a real meal the entire six days they were together. She'd been too infatuated to think of food and her stomach, like the rest of her, had swirled in a constant state of fluttering excitement.

It had been February and a cold front had moved in. They'd stayed inside and nibbled on cheese and crackers for energy. Once after making love, they'd cooked pancakes as the sun was coming up. Dakota had spilled flour down his bare chest and it had stuck like snowflakes on his dark hairs.

She had a sudden craving for pancakes now. Fortunately, they weren't on the luncheon menu. Instead she ordered a grilled chicken salad. Dakota ordered a porterhouse steak with a baked potato.

She'd barely nibbled at her meal and Dakota was half-through with his when a reed-thin young woman with punky red highlights in her black hair entered the restaurant. She wore oversize sunglasses, tight denim shorts and a white cotton shirt that was so big it fell off her narrow shoulders. Her belly had a swell to it that indicated she was a few months pregnant.

"Ten to one that's your girl Shelby," Dakota said.

"I'm inclined to agree with you. She doesn't

look like your typical steakhouse clientele, especially for this neighborhood."

Viviana stood and waved so that Shelby would see them tucked away in a back booth. Shelby put her head down, crossed the room and stopped near Viviana. A tissue clutched in her hand was twisted into shreds.

"You must be Shelby," Viviana said.

"Yes. And you're Dr. Mancini. I recognize you from a picture that Hank has." Shelby's voice was as shaky and unsure as she seemed.

"Hank carries my picture around?"

"Not exactly, but he has it at the house."

Not comforting. "I would think he had better things to do with his time."

"He just doesn't want to go back to jail."

He should have thought of that before he started shaking Leslie Compton, Viviana thought. She kept that to herself. No use upsetting Shelby any more than she already was, especially before she heard what the woman had come to say.

Viviana kept her tone congenial. "Did you have trouble finding the restaurant?"

"No. I knew where it was. I used to date one of the cooks. That was a few years back."

"Dr. Mancini told me about your brother,"

Dakota said, breaking into the conversation. "I'm sorry for your loss. This must be a very difficult time for you."

"It's hard. Kevin had problems, with drugs, you know. He liked to get high. But he never hurt anyone. He didn't deserve to get shot."

"Do you have any idea why someone shot him?" Dakota asked.

Shelby finally looked up to face Dakota. "Are you a cop or a lawyer or something?"

"Nope. I'm just a cowboy."

"You ask questions like a cop. Anyway, I didn't come here to talk about Kevin."

"So tell me about Hank Bateman," Viviana said. "How do you know him?"

"I'm his woman."

Obviously post Karen Compton. "How long have the two of you been together?"

"Ever since Karen dumped him. I stood by him."

"Hasn't he been in jail most of that time?"

"Yeah, but we still talked. His friends looked out for me while he was locked up."

"Looked out for" most likely meant supplied her with drugs. Now she was emaciated, unsteady and fearful…and probably barely out of her teens.

"What is it that you feel I should know about Hank?"

"He didn't kill that baby. He wasn't even home that night."

"He brought her to the hospital," Viviana reminded her.

"I know but that was because he came back and found her like that."

Shelby was either extremely naive or lying. Or else Hank Bateman had brainwashed her.

"That's between Hank and the police, Shelby. All I can testify is the condition of Leslie Compton when she was admitted to the E.R."

The waitress stopped by to see if Shelby was joining them for lunch.

"Nothing for me," Shelby said.

"Are you sure?" Dakota asked. "You might feel better if you eat. My treat."

"No. I couldn't keep anything down, what with Kevin getting killed. A diet cola would be good, though."

The waitress nodded and left a napkin for Shelby.

Shelby smoothed the cotton square with her fingertips, rubbing so hard the pressure against the plastic counter made a squeaking noise. "Don't testify against Hank, Dr. Mancini. Please, just tell the attorney you changed you mind."

"Did Hank ask you to talk to me?"

"No, and he wouldn't like it if he knew I was here. Please don't tell him."

"Did you ask Karen Compton not to testify? Is that why she left town?"

"No. I thought…" She shook her head, her eyes downcast. "I didn't know she'd left town. I haven't seen her in months."

"But you know her."

"We were friends once. She doesn't have anything to do with me since Hank took me for his girlfriend."

"Maybe she just doesn't want to be around Hank since he killed her baby," Viviana said. "Maybe you should think about finding someone else to be with, too. What if he took a notion to shake your baby to death?"

Shelby started to shake. "He wouldn't hurt his own kid. He's not like that. Please, just tell the attorney you changed your mind and they'd probably just call off the trial."

"I can't do that, Shelby. I have to testify and I have to tell the truth about what I know. I won't be cajoled or frightened out of it. I have to do what's right."

"If something happens… Well, just remember that I begged you not to. I have to go now, but don't tell anyone I talked to you, especially not Detective Cortez."

"I take it you've met the detective."

"Yes, he came by this morning to tell me about Kevin getting killed. He even tried to blame that on Hank, but I know Hank didn't do it."

"What makes you so sure?"

"Hank was with me last night."

"What time did you talk to Detective Cortez?"

"Early this morning, around eight."

That was before the detective had turned up at Viviana's house, yet Cortez had indicated he had no idea what Kevin Lucas was referring to when he mumbled *Shell.*

Detective Cortez was the one person she'd trusted to level with her. Now she had to wonder if she could even rely on him.

"Did the detective say who he thought killed your brother?"

"No, but I think he's the one who came to

tell me about his death because he's talked to me before about Hank."

The waitress returned with the drink, but Shelby ignored it in her hurry to leave.

"She's a wreck," Dakota said as he watched Shelby bump into and almost knock over a chair on her way out.

"She's scared, but I don't know if she's afraid for me or for Hank."

"I think she's afraid for you," Dakota said.

"How can you tell?"

"Just a hunch. Have you thought about backing out?"

"And let Hank Bateman get away with murdering that helpless infant? I couldn't live with myself if I did that."

"I understand, but if Bateman is behind everything that happened last night, he's a dangerous lunatic. Which means you're stuck with me for eight more days, so we might as well work at being friends again."

"We were never friends, Dakota. We were madly infatuated lovers from practically the moment we met."

"We could always give that a try."

"You can barely move."

"Then we can at least be civil to each other,

which means no more locking yourself away upstairs as if being near me is going to contaminate you. We're parents. We should at least be able to talk."

"Deal," she agreed.

And for eight days she'd go through the torment of being near Dakota without touching him. Hearing him in the shower without joining him. Sleeping in the same house without crawling into his arms.

Eight days of agony in order to keep Briana safe while not falling helplessly in love with the wrong man all over again.

The trial could not come too soon.

THE SUN WAS LOW in the sky by the time they'd picked up Briana from Claire's, stopped at the market for a few groceries and driven back to Viviana's town house. Dakota hadn't complained but Viviana could tell he was still in significant pain. He was constantly rubbing his right shoulder and she'd seen him wince over nothing more that hitting a rough spot in the road. Worse, he cringed at times just trying to take a deep breath.

"I have some pain meds," she said as he

pulled into her driveway. "You need to take two tablets and go to bed."

"Does that mean I'm no longer relegated to the couch?"

"I'll have to change the sheets but then you can have Claire's room."

"Is that your best offer?"

"Dakota, don't—"

"I know. I know," Dakota interrupted. "I was just trying to inject a little levity into what has been a harrowing day for both of us. You need to relax a little, too. If I say I'll protect you, I will."

He killed the engine and climbed out of the truck.

He'd made a valid point. Why couldn't she just relax and accept his protection? She was the one who'd ended their relationship and he'd merely stayed away as she'd asked. She was the one who hadn't found a way to get word to him that he was a father.

But she couldn't relax around him, would never be able to joke about his coming to her bed. The memories of their time together were too potent. The attraction between them was still far too dynamic.

She got out of the truck, opened the back door and began to unbuckle Briana from her car seat.

"Let me help you with her," he said.

"I don't think you should be lifting yet."

"Briana doesn't weigh much more than those ice packs you keep pushing on me."

"You'd be surprised. But if you insist on trying, I'll get the groceries."

"I'd forgotten about those."

"I can handle them. I'm used to it. Just don't try to pick up Briana with your right arm."

"You got it, Doc."

Viviana snagged the bag of groceries, then waited while Dakota removed Briana from her car seat. The darling kicked a few times in protest. Then she dropped her head to his shoulder, as if it were the most natural thing in the world for this cowboy with a smile that matched her own to be carrying her into the house.

Briana would easily learn to love Dakota, but could he love her back? Would she be able to count on him or would he provide only broken promises and rejection? Would she grow up believing there was something wrong with her that kept him from loving her?

Viviana pulled her new set of door keys from her handbag and hurried to unlock the door. She noticed the doll almost at once, at the edge of the walkway next to a pot of blooming mandevilla. It wasn't Briana's and it hadn't been there when they'd left.

Apprehension made her palms clammy as she stooped to pick up the plastic-and-fabric doll. It wasn't until she'd lifted it that she realized that the back of the doll's head had been crushed. Fake blood dripped down the collar of the doll's delicate sky-blue dress.

This was pathetically sick. She started to slam it back to the walk. That's when she spotted the square of paper tucked inside the doll's cotton panties.

Carefully maneuvering the groceries to free her fingers, she retrieved the note and began to read. The words blurred. Her hands began to shake. And then she felt the earth moving beneath her feet and the walkway rushing toward her face.

Chapter Nine

The diaper bag hadn't been zipped all the way, and when Dakota grabbed the strap to sling it over his free shoulder, two bottles fell and bumped along the driveway before rolling beneath the car. Briana started to wave her hands in the air and do her best to squirm from his hold.

"You think that's funny, do you? I guess you want to crawl under the truck and get them?"

"Duuuuu."

"Chanting won't help, sweetheart. I'm on to you, little Miss Viviana, Jr."

She pushed a thumb into his cheek and smiled. His breath caught and all of a sudden the significance of the moment hit him. He was holding his daughter for the very first time. Not as a newborn, the way most fathers did it, but as a seven-month-old with an attitude and a personality.

She was a real person. She'd have needs. She'd have expectations. Could he be the kind of father she deserved?

You're your father's kid, Dakota. Unless you continuously fight it, the evil will take control of you one day, just like it did him.

He cringed as his uncle's condemning voice echoed in his head.

There was a splat and the sound of breaking glass. Dakota spun around. Viviana was lying on the walkway, her leg twisted beneath her. The bottle of blackberry jam was shattered in jagged shards next to her. Two oranges rolled toward him.

The sights registered as he raced toward Viviana. He knelt down beside her, dropping the diaper bag to the grass and bracing Viviana against him as best he could with Briana's short arms wrapped around his neck.

"Viviana. What happened? Talk to me."

She blinked rapidly and her eyes fluttered open. "Dakota."

"I'm right here. Did you trip? Are you hurt?"

A tinge of color returned to her pasty face.

"No, but I've had all I can take of Hank Bateman." She held up the broken doll as if it were evidence to justify her statement.

"Did you trip over the doll?" He hadn't a clue what that had to do with Hank.

"Read the note." Viviana's voice was shaky. She pushed a small square of paper into Dakota's hand.

Briana began to cry and reach for her mother.

"I'll take her," Viviana said.

"Okay, but don't try to stand with her. And watch for the broken glass." Dakota handed Briana over and read the scribbled words.

Testify and your daughter's head will match the doll's.

Viviana was right. This time Hank Bateman had gone too far.

"BRIANA'S DOWN for the night. At least I hope she is. Can we talk?"

"Sure." As long as it wasn't about the relationship they no longer had. Dakota looked up from the beer he'd been drinking as Viviana entered the kitchen.

They were practically the first words Viviana had spoken since Dirty Harry had left. He'd come over to examine the doll and had taken it and the note with him. Since then, Viviana had been upstairs with Briana, not to avoid him this time, but just to regroup.

That left him alone to stew about what he could do to stop Hank Bateman, short of cracking the back of *his* skull. That possibility was steadily gaining favor.

"How about a beer?" he offered. "Or maybe something stronger?"

"A beer would be good." Viviana slid into a kitchen chair.

He took a beer from the refrigerator and set it in front of her before getting another for himself.

"I've made a decision."

Viviana's somber tone made him edgy. He remained standing. "Let's hear it."

"I'm leaving town."

He hadn't expected that. "What about your job?"

"I have vacation time banked, and I've been granted approval to take it starting as soon as my break is over. Even if I didn't have the time coming, it wouldn't matter. Briana is my life. I have to protect her at any cost."

"Have you given any thought to where you want to go?"

"I have." Viviana took a sip of the beer. "My dad has a sister who lives in a small Texas town not too far from here but off the beaten path."

"Are the two of you close?"

"Closer than I am to anyone else in my family. She pretty much held me together when my mother died. She even took care of the funeral details and paid for everything. She said I'd need the little money Mother had left after her illness for med school."

"I can see why you'd think of her at a time like this."

"Mother didn't stay in touch with any of Dad's family after the divorce. Apparently, neither did Dad. Aunt Abby hasn't heard from him in years. She thinks he may have moved to Mexico."

"Does that mean you never hear from him, either?"

"That's exactly what I mean. I used to receive a Christmas card once a year. Now I don't even get that."

There were obviously enough dysfunctional families to go around.

"Does she know why you're coming?"

"I told her everything. I thought that was only fair. She offered to drive down and pick me up, but I told her you'd drive me. Not that you have to. My insurance will cover a rental car."

"I thought we'd agreed that I could protect you here."

"That was before the doll. I'm not making light of your offer, Dakota. This just seems the better solution to the problem for both of us."

"You might have given me a vote."

"That would have only complicated matters. Aunt Abby has a small house, but she said she'll make room for me and Briana. She even has a neighbor whose kid just outgrew his baby bed. She's going to borrow it for Briana to use."

So that was the plan. Ditch him and turn to the aunt. His blood began to boil. Viviana's life might be hers to do with as she pleased, but Briana was his daughter. He had a say in keeping her safe.

"If dear Aunt Abby only has one extra bed, you better hope it's big enough for two."

She looked at him as if he were speaking Greek. "That's just the point, Dakota. If I'm with Aunt Abby, you won't feel compelled to stick around to protect us."

"I never said I was compelled. I just made that choice. And your aunt may be as good and as trustworthy as gold, but she's no match for Hank Bateman."

"She won't have to be. Hank will never look for me there. No one in San Antonio even knows I have an aunt. Besides, you said the first time we were together that you lost your edge if you stayed away from bull riding for any extended period of time."

"We're only talking about a week. Once the trial is over, either Hank goes free or he's locked up for years. Either way, the need to keep you from testifying becomes a moot point."

"If you really want to go with us, I suppose that can be arranged."

"Is there another man in your life? Is that why you're so hell-bent on ditching me?"

"No. I told you there's been no one since

you. When would I have had time for a man even if I'd wanted one?"

He picked up his beer. "Then what's the name of this safe little town where the three of us will crowd in on poor Aunt Abby?"

"Mustang Run."

Dakota choked on his beer. Viviana jumped up, grabbed a couple of napkins off the counter and handed one to Dakota. While he dabbed the sputtered liquid from his chin and the front of his shirt, she wiped off the counter.

"Are you okay?" she asked.

"Not with this plan. You can just forget about Mustang Run. We are not going there."

"Why? What do you have against Mustang Run? Aunt Abby says it's a charming town. And the sheriff is one of her best friends. She said he'll be there in a matter of minutes if I need him for anything at all."

"If you want to disappear, you need a big city. We can drive to Dallas or fly to Chicago or even New York. I'll take care of expenses. It will be like a vacation."

And if he decided to return to the bull-riding circuit or if he got tired of being the protective father he claimed he didn't know how to be, she and Briana would be stranded in a strange town where they knew no one. Besides, he hadn't objected to a small town until she'd mentioned Mustang Run by name.

"Give me one good reason why I shouldn't go to Mustang Run," she demanded.

He exhaled slowly. "Troy Ledger."

"What does that mean?"

"You asked for one good reason. I just gave it to you. It's Troy Ledger."

"Who—or what—is Troy Ledger?"

"My infamous father. You must be the only person in Texas who hasn't heard of him."

Viviana was certain Dakota had never mentioned any of his family. Another of the problems with jumping headlong into a week of devouring each other. Between the chocolate and whipped cream and myriad other sexual experiences so hot and exciting they had blown her mind, she and Dakota had passed right over all the normal relationship preliminaries.

"What's Troy Ledger's claim to infamy?"

"He was sentenced to life in prison."

"On what charges?"

"Murdering my mother."

It took a few seconds for the shock to settle. "I had no idea. I'm so sorry."

"Don't be. It was a long time ago."

Yet he was clearly still traumatized by it. "Do you want to talk about it?"

"Not much point."

"Have you seen or been in contact with your father since he went to prison?"

"No. The last time I saw him was at his conviction. I'd just turned seven at the time. Before that, I hadn't spoken to him since the day my mother was killed. I haven't until this day, and I'm perfectly happy keeping it that way. I'm not looking for pity. I'm also not looking to reconnect with Troy Ledger."

"Isn't he still in prison?"

"He was released a year ago on a technicality. He returned to the ranch in Mustang Run and is now living in the house where my mother was shot and killed."

"Maybe you should go back to Mustang Run, Dakota. It might give you some closure."

"I'm not looking for closure, and I don't need you to serve as my shrink."

"Do you have other family in Mustang Run?"

"I do now. My brother Dylan and his wife

live on Willow Creek Ranch with my father, though they have their own house. My brother Tyler is in the army and stationed in Afghanistan, but his new bride, Julie, is living on the ranch in a starter house Troy, Dylan and Sean built for her and Tyler."

"Who's Sean?"

"Another brother. He's a horse whisperer. He married Dad's prison psychiatrist and they bought a horse farm in Bandera."

"How many brothers do you have?"

"Four. Wyatt's a homicide detective in Atlanta. He and I are the only two siblings who haven't jumped on the big happy family bandwagon."

She wondered if Wyatt was as bitter as Dakota…and why the others weren't. "Aunt Abby probably knows your father and your brothers. She owns a diner in town, so she knows almost everybody for miles around."

"I'm sure she knows them. Dylan's married to the sheriff's daughter. I'm going with you when you leave here, Viviana. So pick any town other than Mustang Run."

"I can't, Dakota. It's all arranged. I'll feel safe there and I'm close enough to come back to San Antonio if the prosecutor needs me for any reason. And if the hospital falls into a serious bind due to some kind of catastrophe or natural disaster, I could leave Briana with Abby and return to work, even sleep at the hospital if I think it's necessary."

Those were all valid reasons, but just as importantly, she was getting an uncanny premonition that they were meant to go to Mustang Run. "If three of your brothers have reconnected with Troy Ledger, then it can't kill you to at least make a visit home, Dakota."

"I have no home."

He turned his back on her and walked away. For the first time, she'd glimpsed a part of Dakota that lived beneath his almost impenetrable shell. He was more vulnerable than he wanted anyone to know.

It changed things between them, connected them in ways the initial spontaneous and fevered attraction hadn't. They could never go to back to the purely physical relationship, to desire so primal it defied reason.

That didn't mean they couldn't move on to something even better.

But she definitely wasn't counting on that.

DAKOTA STRETCHED OUT on the bed that un-officially belonged to the nanny. It was far more accommodating of his size than the sofa had been, but there was still no way to get comfortable.

He was used to aches and pains. It went with the bull-riding territory. Some days it was worse than others. Today it was a killer. Thank God he'd been wearing the protective vest.

Truth was, though, that it wasn't the soreness that had him tense and edgy. It was everything coming down on him at once. Running into Viviana and finding her in danger. Learning he was a father. Actually holding a beautiful baby born of his own seed.

His seed. The Ledger legacy.

You're cursed, Dakota Ledger. You got a killer's blood running through your veins.

His uncle's words echoed through his mind as they had so many times before. At six, they'd terrified him. That was before he'd learned what real terror was.

His cell phone vibrated, making a clacking sound against the wooden nightstand. He grabbed the phone quickly before the noise woke Briana.

"Yo."

"Dakota, hi, it's Dylan."

Dread swelled inside him. Surely Dylan hadn't already heard he'd be in Mustang Run tomorrow. "What's up?"

"We heard you got thrown hard last night and ended up in the hospital."

"Bad news travels fast."

"It did this time. You were mentioned in the morning newspaper."

"Must be a slow news day for the sports-writers."

"How bad were you hurt?"

"I've got a few bruised ribs and a sprained right shoulder. Nothing that won't heal itself in a few days."

"Good. Dad saw it and he got worried."

Sure he did. "You can tell him I'm fine. I'll take a few days to heal and then I'll be back on the bulls."

"Since you are so close and not competing for a few days, why not spend that time here at the ranch? I'd love for you to see what we've done with the spread. And we have two new colts that were foaled last month."

"I'd love to see you and the horses, and meet your wife, but I need to stick close this week in case I need some physical therapy."

"Is this about therapy or about Dad?"

No use to deny the truth. "You know how I feel about him."

"Bitterness is a heavy load to tote through life, Dakota."

"Don't get preachy on me."

"Okay, but I think you're making a mistake in not giving Dad a chance."

"It won't be my first one."

"So how about I drive over to San Antonio and meet you for lunch? We're brothers. We should be able to talk."

"Maybe next time. I've got business that needs taking care of."

"If you change your mind, I'd love to see you. We all would."

"If I change my mind, I'll call."

And look out for the ice storm if he did, 'cause hell would surely be freezing over.

DAKOTA HAD PULLED his truck into the garage when he started loading it for the trip to Mustang Run. On the outside chance someone was watching the house, there was no point in announcing they were leaving town.

He'd packed his one bag into the truck first, glad he'd made use of Viviana's washer and dryer last night to launder his lucky red shirt and the rest of his dirty clothes.

Next he lifted the cooler with Briana's bottles into the backseat of the truck and then slung two huge suitcases into the truck bed.

"I told you to let me put that luggage in the car," Viviana protested as she rolled out yet another bag.

"I used the good shoulder."

"Well, get out of the way, because I intend to put this one in the truck myself."

"Are you planning on changing clothes every five minutes?"

"No, but sometimes Briana does. Plus I have to take her bottles and food and diapers and toys and—"

"Bricks," Dakota added. "I'm sure that brown carry-on is full of bricks."

"Books from my TBR pile. I haven't finished a book since Briana was born. A week in exile should give me a chance to do that. And my weights are in there. I have to stay in shape and there's no time for the gym with Briana around."

Gym or not, whatever Viviana was doing worked. She'd added a few pounds since he'd seen her last, but they looked good on her. He was pretty sure her breasts were a little bigger, too. He'd know if…

The image of her naked slipped into his mind. He shook his head to clear it. Start thinking like that and he'd get so worked up it would make driving all but impossible.

"I need to make one last trip through the house to make sure everything is turned off and all the doors and windows are locked," Viviana said. "Then I'll get Briana from her playpen and we'll be ready to roll. Except that I need to fold the playpen and put it in the truck. Oh, no. I almost forgot her jump chair. That's a lifesaver when she gets too fussy for words."

"Keep going and I'll have to rent a moving van."

Viviana leaned against the truck. "Are you sure you want to do this?" she asked. "There's still time for you to back out."

"I don't relish spending any time in Mustang Run. But I'm not backing out. I'll see this through until the trial is over."

"I just don't want you to think that…" She hesitated.

"To think that this means I can jump your bones."

"I wasn't going to put it that way."

"I believe in telling it straight. I'm not looking for a roll in the hay as thanks, Viviana. When and if we ever make love again, it will be because we both want it. We've had delirious perfection. Duty sex won't cut it."

"You do believe in telling it straight."

Ten minutes later, they were buckled in and backing out of the driveway. A car pulled up behind them, blocking them in.

"The return of Dirty Harry," Dakota said. "Did you tell him you were leaving town?"

"No, but I guess I will now. I'd planned to give him a call later."

"Since he doesn't know you're leaving, I guess he's not just dropping by to say adios."

Dakota and Viviana both got out of the truck while Detective Cortez lumbered toward them.

The detective glared at Dakota. "I see you're still here."

Dakota decided against the first smart-ass reply that popped into his mind and settled on something slightly less obnoxious. "Do you have a problem with that?"

"Not as long as I don't have to do business with you."

"Did you find my car?" Viviana asked.

"Yep, we did. That's the good news. Now for the bad."

Chapter Ten

"Your car is totaled," Cortez said. "An off-duty police officer spotted a flume of black smoke off a dirt road near his fishing camp about ten miles west of the city. At first he thought it was just someone burning trash. He checked it out and found the car completely gutted by flames."

"How can you be sure it's mine?"

"The VIN number was still decipherable."

Tears burned at the back of her eyes. This was totally mad. And for what? "I loved that car. I looked for weeks to find just the right color and model. I hadn't even made a payment yet. It was the first non-junky car I'd ever owned in my life."

"I guess that rules out any chance of the vehicle providing fingerprints," Dakota said.

The detective nodded.

Briana began to fuss in her car seat. She'd start to scream any minute if they didn't get moving. Viviana felt that same urge.

"Why steal my car only to set it on fire? If Hank Bateman is responsible for this, his actions are having just the opposite effect of what he intends. This makes me more determined than ever to see him in prison. It's where that lunatic belongs."

"There's no proof he's behind it. He definitely didn't set the car on fire himself."

"How can you be so sure?" Dakota asked.

"We have a tail on him."

"Your car was set on fire sometime during the night and Hank hasn't left his house since yesterday afternoon."

"What time yesterday?"

"Somewhere around 3:00 p.m."

That left Hank plenty of time to drop off the doll and the note before his movements were being monitored.

Harry Cortez stretched his arms out in front of him, then relaxed them and popped his large, knotty knuckles. "There's more."

"Oh, joy." The wisecrack fell flat. Frustration was making her ill.

"The charred remains of a body were found in the front seat."

Viviana closed her eyes and tried to obliterate the sickening image that filled her head. Being an emergency medicine specialist, she'd seen her share of victims of gruesome accidents. That didn't make the image of a fatally burned body any easier to swallow.

Dakota wrapped a steadying arm around her waist. "Has the victim been identified?"

"Not yet. It may take several days. The M.E. will likely need a dental record match."

"Male or female?" Dakota asked.

"Male. The M.E. could tell that much."

"Not likely that the thief set the car on fire and then got back in it," Dakota said.

"Not likely," the detective admitted. "We'll know more when we get the autopsy."

"This makes absolutely no sense," Viviana said. "I go months without threats of any kind, then all of a sudden, horrors are pounding me like ice in a hailstorm."

"We'll get to the bottom of it," Cortez said. "In the meantime, I'm requesting an officer be assigned to protect you. It's either that or have you checked into a safe house. That can be pretty complicated when it involves a baby as young as yours. It can be done, though. In fact, the chief may order it."

"She has a bodyguard," Dakota said before she had a chance to answer.

"You? A rodeo jockey?"

"That's right."

"Face it, Ledger. Viviana needs a professional in charge of her protection."

"I appreciate the offer of protection," Viviana said, "but right now, I'll stick with Dakota."

The detective's expression said it all. He thought she was making a big mistake. If she was, Briana's safety would also be at risk.

But so far Dakota had a winning record. He'd saved her life two out of two times. If she'd gotten into the car with that gunman, her body might have been the one found burned to a crisp. If Dakota hadn't chased off the man at her window, he'd have gotten inside her house where she, Briana and Claire would have been at his mercy.

"Call me if you change your mind," Cortez said. He turned to walk away.

She started to shake. Dakota pulled her into his arms and held her close until the shudders ripping through her settled into a numbing stillness.

Crazy, but in spite of all the times she'd thrilled at Dakota's touch, she'd never realized how safe it felt just to have his arms around her.

DAKOTA PARKED IN the center of the old downtown section of Mustang Run at ten minutes after one in the afternoon. From the looks of things, they'd time traveled back to the early days of the preceding century. Only instead of honky-tonks and livery stables, the one-story buildings housed small boutiques, antique shops, an ice-cream emporium, a tempting bakery and, of course, Abby's Diner.

"Just in time for lunch," Viviana said.

Dakota turned the key and killed the engine. "The sign says home cooking and fresh-baked pies. I can go for both of those." He might as well try to keep a positive spin on the whole Mustang Run adventure until it turned sour on him.

Viviana had Briana out of her seat by the time he rounded the back of the truck. "Smelly time," she said. "Can you grab the diaper bag for me? There should be a changing station in the ladies' restroom."

He retrieved it, flicked the lock button on his key and followed them inside. It didn't look like the kind of town where you needed to lock doors, but he was taking no chances.

The odors, boisterous voices and clattering of dishes attacked as the bell over the door announced their entrance. Dakota glanced at the crowded counter, where an eclectic mixture of businessmen in suits and ranchers in jeans were immersed in their meals. Several were digging into mouthwatering piles of meringue.

"If the food tastes as good as it smells and looks, I'm destined to gain a few pounds around Aunt Abby," Dakota said.

"The smell I'm getting is not that appetizing," Viviana said. "But I am hungry and thirsty. Why don't you snare that empty booth near the window? If the waitress stops by, order me a diet cola while I change Briana."

"You got it. When do we meet the illustrious Aunt Abby?"

"She's probably in the kitchen. I'll check when I get back."

Dakota claimed the booth and then turned

his concentration to the food being served by hustling waitresses. A plate of chicken and dumplings with sides of greens and fried okra looked tempting. So did a tray carrying a plate that spilled over with a huge chicken-fried steak topped by a mountain of cream gravy, all cozied up next to a mound of sliced beefsteak tomatoes.

He scanned the men at the counter with a more discerning eye. No one looked even vaguely familiar, not that he'd expect them to. Nor would he look familiar to them. He'd changed a lot since age six. If he kept a very low profile, maybe he'd actually make it through the week without his family knowing he was around.

A whiff of fried catfish had him practically drooling. His gaze followed the waitress carrying the tray of golden brown filets and crispy French fries.

She stopped at his booth. "I'll be right with you. Today's specials are listed on the board over the counter, but I'll bring menus."

Dakota scrutinized the rest of the customers. The waitress served the catfish to a man reading the newspaper in a booth across from the door to the restroom.

The man looked up as she set the plate in front of him. He ignored her. Instead his penetrating gaze fixed on Dakota.

Dakota's mouth went dry. A roar filled his head, as deafening as the tornado he'd lived through when he was ten. He watched, muscles clenched, as Troy Ledger stood and started walking toward him.

There was no doubt it was him. Dylan had sent a picture of the three forgiving brothers and Troy via cell phone. Even if he hadn't seen the picture, Dakota would have recognized Troy. The Ledger features that were so prominent in him were also undeniable in Dakota and his brothers.

Dakota slid from the booth as Troy extended a hand.

"You were the last person I expected to run into in Abby's," Troy said.

The same was true for Dakota. Otherwise, he wouldn't be here.

"For a few seconds there, I was afraid to believe my eyes," Troy continued. His voice was husky with emotion.

Dakota swallowed hard. He so did not need this. "It's a spur-of-the-moment trip," he offered.

"That works. I'm just glad you changed your mind about driving over for a visit."

"Actually, I'm not really here to visit."

His father looked hurt, or maybe just confused.

"I'm in Mustang Run to take care of some business," Dakota said.

"What kind of business?"

"Personal."

"I see. Does that mean you weren't going to call and tell your brothers or me that you were in town?"

"I wasn't sure I'd have time for visiting." That wasn't a total lie, but it felt like one.

Troy worried an old scar that dominated the right side of his face. "Then I guess I'm lucky I ran into you here."

Great reunion they were having so far. Dakota had no idea what Troy expected of him. Whatever it was, he couldn't deliver. His right shoulder began to throb. He massaged the painful area.

"Looks like you're having trouble with that arm. The newspaper said you got roughed up pretty bad a couple of nights ago," Troy said.

"Reporters tend to exaggerate."

Thankfully, a waitress approached. She

didn't have menus, but she did have a gleam in her eye. She flashed a smile that lit up her plump face as she caught hold of Troy's arm.

"Glory be and bringing in the sheaves. Tell me my eyes are not lying, Troy Ledger. This has got to be Dakota." She wiped her hands on the front of a bleached white apron.

Before Dakota could react, the matronly woman pulled him into a hug. Then she backed away and looked him over as if he were a breed bull she was thinking of buying.

"I swear you look just like your dad did at your age."

"You say that about all my sons," Troy said.

"Well, they do. I'm Abby," she said. "I know you don't remember me, Dakota, but I sure remember you. You hit me with a spitball one day in church, you little stinker. But you sure grew up nice. That you did. A darn good bull rider, too, I hear. Helene would be proud as punch of all her boys."

"Aunt Abby."

"Ba ba ga ma."

Viviana and Briana pushed into the awkward circle. It was too late to run. The party Dakota had hoped to avoid was now in full swing.

TROY STRUGGLED TO get a handle on his emotions. Dakota was actually here, standing less than a foot from him. Not the mischievous little kid who'd made them laugh with his nonstop antics. Not the boy who could make Helene cry with a bouquet of weeds picked from the yard and a sticky hug around the neck.

He was a man now. There was so much Troy needed to say to him, but it would be a waste of time. Dakota wore his resentment on his sleeve, more obvious than a tattoo, more cutting than a Bowie knife.

And Abby was going on and on, gushing over some cute, jabbering kid and preventing any chance Troy had for a conversation with the son he hadn't seen in eighteen years.

"Have you met Dakota?"

Troy studied the woman who'd asked the question. She looked like a model for one of those slick women's fashion magazines. Flawless olive complexion. Dark, curly hair that tumbled around her slender shoulders. Long, dark lashes that outlined the most expressive eyes he'd seen in many a moon.

"I've known Dakota Ledger since he was born," Abby said. "I grew up with his mother, grade school right through high school. I've been knowing Troy since he came into town and swept Helene right off her feet. 'Course they both dropped out of my life for many a year."

"So you're Troy Ledger," the young woman said. She eyed him warily. He was used to that from strangers. It went with the murder conviction.

"I'm Troy Ledger."

"I'm Viviana Mancini. I'm very glad to meet you." Her circumspection transformed into a smile.

Abby coochie-cooed the baby and then looked back to its stunning mother. "How do you know Dakota?"

"He's the friend I told you I was bringing with me."

"Well if this old world isn't shrinking to the size of a dried-up walnut. I never dreamed Dakota Ledger was the friend you were talking about."

Troy looked at Viviana's ring finger. It was bare, which didn't necessarily mean anything these days. He hoped that Dakota's business wasn't rendezvousing in Mustang Run with a married woman who had a young kid.

"I need to finish up a couple of things in the kitchen while you kids get something to eat. Then I'll run you over to my place so you can get settled in," Abby said. She reached over and rustled the baby's thick, dark curls. "And you, Miss Briana Mancini, can have a nice long nap so you can be wide-awake to play with your great-aunt Abby when I get home tonight."

Viviana looked Troy square in the eye. "Actually, it's Briana Marie Ledger."

Shock left Troy speechless. He looked to Dakota, but his son was staring at Viviana as if she'd just committed treason. He glanced at the dark-haired baby. There were resemblances.

"Are you saying that Briana is my grandchild?"

The couple in front of them turned to stare. That was the least of Troy's concerns.

Dakota straightened and finally met Troy's gaze. "Yes, Briana's my daughter."

"Don't that beat all?" Abby said. "My grandniece is a Ledger." She punched Troy in the arm. "We're practically kin."

"It looks that way." Troy got a funny feeling

in his chest. He stared at the baby. Amazed. And suddenly enchanted.

"If you're here with Dakota, then why in the world do you want to be cooped up in my little house?" Abby asked. "Not that I'm not glad to have you but Troy's got a big, rambling house out there on Willow Creek Ranch. And you'd have at least three tough cowboys to protect you and Briana from that baby killer back in San Antonio."

Troy's ire fired like an explosion. "What's this about a baby killer?"

Now everyone in the restaurant was starting to stare.

"I think we'd best finish this conversation in the kitchen," Abby said.

"Anyone who tries to hurt my granddaughter better have his will made out."

VIVIANA KNEW SHE hadn't played fair. She might feel a lot guiltier about that had it not been for the body that had burned along with her car. Hank Bateman might not have lit the fire himself, but he was behind it. It was the kind of act she'd expect from a man sick enough to kill a helpless infant.

Dakota was strong, tough and willing to

protect her and Briana, but he was only one man. She liked the odds a whole lot better with four Ledgers to fight off the bad guys.

If there was more to her reasoning, she wasn't admitting it yet. But she had liked Troy from almost the minute she'd met him. So had Briana, and babies were seldom fooled. Dakota might not need a father, but Briana could use a doting grandfather and she'd never get that from Viviana's dad.

"Do we have much farther to go?" she asked.

"About five miles." Dakota kept both hands on the steering wheel and didn't glance her way.

"Are you going to pout and not speak to me the whole time we're on the ranch?"

"Don't tell me you're going to start worrying about my feelings now."

"Staying at the ranch makes sense and you know it, Dakota. We'll each have our own bedroom, even Briana. We'll be on an isolated ranch with no one around to see and identify us in case Hank Bateman or one of his henchmen happens to come snooping around."

"And I'll get to roam the house where my

mother was murdered. We'll just have a jolly old time."

Viviana had been so focused on doing what was best for Briana, she hadn't even considered that. Guilt set in, causing her to rethink her impulsive decision. "I'm sorry, Dakota. If you don't want to stay at the ranch, turn around and we'll go back to Abby's. That was our original agreement. I had no right to change it against your will."

He nudged his Stetson back an inch or two. "No. You were right. The ranch makes more sense and I was probably going to have to face my dad one day just to get my brothers off my back. It may as well be now."

"You might consider giving him a chance. Innocent men have been convicted before. Your father could be telling the truth."

"He's definitely convinced Dylan, Tyler and Sean that he is."

"And they know him a lot better than you do," she reminded him.

"Okay, I concede that he might be innocent. Are you happy now?"

"If you think he might be innocent, then I don't see why you're so dead set against at least trying to reconnect with him."

"He doesn't need me. And I don't need him. That's just how it is."

"But not how it has to be."

Dakota turned into a dirt drive and stopped at a metal gate. The sign hanging above it read Welcome to Willow Creek Ranch. A large black crow set atop the sign. It cawed loudly, almost as if it were warning her to stay out.

A shiver crept up Viviana's spine. What if she'd been wrong in insisting they come here? Evil had visited this ranch the day Helene Ledger had been brutally murdered. What if it came again?

She was being foolishly superstitious now. Evil didn't hang around like a ghost waiting until the perfect victim came its way.

Hank Bateman was the only evil she had to worry about, and it was extremely unlikely he'd show up here. If he did, the Ledgers could handle him. Actually, Dakota probably could singlehandedly take care of a rat like Hank.

But why take that chance? Why risk Dakota's life when all the backup he needed was waiting right here on the ranch he refused to call home?

"THIS IS THE GUEST ROOM," Troy said. "Helene planned this wing of the house. The master bedroom is right on the other side of that courtyard garden. That was Helene's favorite spot. Dakota used to take his dump truck out there and move dirt around. Told us he was fertilizing."

The house held few memories for Dakota. Either he'd been too young when his mother had died or else he'd blocked them from his consciousness. He stepped back into the hallway.

Viviana seemed fascinated by the house's history. He doubted either of them would miss him.

He wandered back down the hallway and paused at a closed door. Impulsively, he opened it and stepped into the room. Finally the familiarity spurred a few haunting memories. This had been his room. The twin bed next to the window had been his bed. He'd kept all his treasures in the bottom drawer of that old pine dresser. He'd even put a little grass snake in there once.

He ran his finger along the back edge of the dresser until he felt a small niche. He'd carved it there with Wyatt's scout knife.

Wyatt had found him with the knife and told him he'd be in big trouble if his mother found out he was playing with knives and cutting up furniture. Wyatt had never told on him.

Odd that he remembered something as mundane as that when he couldn't remember anything about his mother's murder. He didn't really remember her, but he knew what she looked like.

His grandmother had made sure of that. She'd given him a scrapbook of pictures of him with his mother so that he'd never forget her. He'd slept with that scrapbook under his pillow for years.

There was something else behind the old chest. He could feel it with his fingertips but couldn't tell what it was. Pain seared through his chest as he scooted the heavy wood furniture away from the wall. Oddly, the pain was a relief. It brought his focus back to the present.

The object was nothing but a book. He stooped and picked it up. *Mike Mulligan and His Steam Shovel*. Just a kid's book, but as fast as quicksilver a memory leaped from the crevices where it had been in hiding.

His mother had read that book to him over and over. She'd try to talk him into something else, but he'd always wanted Mike. He couldn't have been more than three years old then.

A mother who read to you. Brothers who played with you and helped keep you out of trouble. A ranch to explore. Horses to ride. A father to teach you guy things.

That was the life he would have had if his mother had lived. Dakota's chest tightened and hot flashes of pain slashed at the muscles around his rib cage. The tension was adding strain to the injured areas. Riding bulls would be easier than facing this.

He stuck his hat back on his head, walked to the kitchen and out the back door. He needed fresh air and space to breathe.

TROY TIGHTENED the last bolt. "All done. The crib is ready for Briana. It's a good thing Abby found one because there's none in my attic. We got rid of it after Dakota outgrew it. He was the caboose."

"Dakota has issues with you," Viviana said, for some reason thinking she should explain his walking out without saying a word to either of them.

"He has reason to," Troy said. "I'd probably feel the same if I was in his place. Don't apologize for him. He'll come around if and when he's ready."

"Okay." Viviana shook out the nice clean crib sheet and fit it on the mattress. "This bed is in great shape."

"Louella had five grandchildren. She probably bought it new when the first one came along."

"I'm glad she's not using it now."

"I could use a cup of coffee," Troy said. "How about you? I could make some fresh."

"I'm not much of a coffee drinker after that first cup in the morning, but I'd love a diet soda if you have one."

"So happens I do. Sean's wife, Eve, is a soda drinker."

"Let me check on Briana and I'll meet you in the kitchen," Viviana said.

As Troy gathered up his tools, Viviana walked back to the cozy bedroom with the garden view. Briana was fast asleep in her playpen. Maybe she knew she was safe on her grandfather's hill country ranch. Viviana was even beginning to relax herself.

Her soda was open and waiting, accompanied by a glass of ice. She drank too many sodas, a habit picked up while she'd been cramming her way through med school. She'd actually been making progress toward cutting back when the Hank Bateman nightmare had started.

Troy poured himself a cup of stale coffee and joined her at the kitchen table. Apparently he'd decided not to bother with making a fresh pot. The conversation they'd started in the bedroom was still bothering her.

"Stop me if you think I'm interfering where I'm not welcome, but I don't think Dakota's issues with you are all about his mother's murder."

"That's good because I didn't kill Helene. I'm innocent on that count."

His tone disturbed her. "Are you guilty of something else?"

"I'm guilty of blind complacency."

"I'm not following you."

"I didn't fight hard enough to prove my innocence. I'm not sure I cared what became of me at the time. I loved Helene so much that when I lost her, I wanted to die. My boys should have been reason enough to fight for my freedom, but I simply couldn't face life without her."

"So you just let them convict you without mounting a defense?"

"I'm not sure I could have turned the tide of suspicion, but, yes, basically, I didn't fight for my freedom. I was so depressed I didn't even cooperate with my attorney. I just clammed up or else I would have gone berserk that no one was finding her killer."

"Dakota said he never heard from you when he was growing up."

"Once the depression and grief became tolerable, I tried to get in touch with the boys. Helene's parents filed a lawsuit claiming they were terrified of me and that contact with me was too upsetting. To tell the truth, I figured the boys were better off with me out of their lives. I was in prison for life. I had nothing to offer. The best thing I could do for them was let them have a normal life."

Briana was only seven months old, but Viviana couldn't imagine going through life and never knowing if she was healthy or sick or if her heart was bursting with happiness or breaking into tiny pieces.

"I can't undo what's done," Troy said. "Dakota is a grown man. He'll make up his own mind about whether or not he wants me in his life, just as my other sons have done. I have no choice but to accept that."

Troy sipped the stale coffee. "So let's talk about something we might be able to do something about. Tell me about this trouble you're having."

She explained as succinctly as she could, filling him in on the gory details.

"Hank Bateman." Troy chewed on the edge of his bottom lip as if deep in thought. "For some reason that name sounds familiar."

"Maybe you've met him. Do you travel to San Antonio often?"

"I haven't been there since my release from… Prison. That's why the name sounds familiar."

"Was Hank in prison with you?"

"Not that I recall, but there was a George Bateman. Big guy. Mean as a snake. Got in a fight once and killed a guy with his bare hands. He said it was self-defense. Nobody who saw it was brave enough to say he was lying."

"Intimidating witnesses. That sounds like Hank, but you said your prison mate was named George."

Troy nodded. "But he talked about a brother and I'm almost sure his name was Hank. I know George was from San Antonio."

"Is George still in prison?"

"No, he was granted parole a good two years before I was released. I can check, see what I can find out about him. I don't see offhand how knowing about George could help you, but more information never hurts."

Viviana looked up at the sound of footsteps at the back door. Dakota stepped inside, took off his hat and tossed it onto a chair. "Am I interrupting anything?"

"No," Troy said. "We were just talking."

"Troy put the crib together," Viviana said.

"Thanks. I was coming in to do that now."

"It was no trouble," Troy said. "Fact is, it was kind of fun. It's the first time we've had a baby around the house since you were born."

"Briana's only here for a week," Dakota quickly reminded him.

"This time," Viviana corrected. "But she'll

come back to visit her grandfather." She knew Dakota's feelings toward Troy, but she thought he was being grossly unfair to the man. Based on first impressions, she liked Troy a lot.

"When do I get to meet the rest of the family?" she asked.

"Tomorrow evening," Troy said. "Family dinner right here. Eve says Joey is so excited about meeting his bull-riding Uncle Dakota that she'll be surprised if he sleeps tonight."

"Joey I haven't heard about," Viviana said.

"That's Sean's stepson. He's seven and a bundle of energy. He'll bring Sparky with him, too. He takes that golden retriever everywhere he goes except church and school."

"I can't wait to meet him."

"There's coffee in the pot and soft drinks and beer in the fridge," Troy offered his son.

"Thanks." Dakota got a beer from the refrigerator but didn't join them at the table. Instead he went back and stood near the back door, staring out at the summer landscape as if he were planning another escape.

"Did you go to Dylan's while you were out?" Viviana asked him.

"No, I just took a short walk to get a breath of fresh air."

Viviana finished her drink as the tension built in the kitchen. Perhaps the men needed time alone. "I should unpack before Briana wakes up. Thanks for the cola, Troy."

"You help yourself to another soda or anything else around here you want. Think of this as home while you're here."

"I appreciate that."

There was dead silence between the two men as Viviana walked away. But at least they were in the same room. That was progress.

She started to unpack, but mean-as-a-snake George Bateman stayed on her mind. If Hank wasn't doing his own dirty work, then maybe his brother George was doing it for him.

She took her cell phone from her purse to call Dirty Harry. He'd know if Hank had a brother who'd been in prison. The display informed her she had received three new messages since she'd arrived at the ranch a few hours earlier.

She called her voice mail, punched in the code and listened to the first message. It was from the detective.

"Hank's still being tailed. He's mostly hanging out with his girlfriend. There's been no sign of trouble and no attempt to flee the area. The cops are monitoring your place. All clear there."

Dirty Harry might not be the neatest of souls, but he appeared to have everything under control. After a year of bureaucracy and postponement, this trial might actually get under way one week from today.

The second message was from Betsy, a nurse in the E.R. She wanted to know why Viviana had taken her vacation on such short notice. Was Viviana all right? Was Briana?

Viviana would text her back later that she was fine. She wouldn't mention she was with the "gorgeous" cowboy Betsy had tended to at the hospital.

The third message was from the prosecuting attorney. Nick Jefferson had bad news.

The nightmare had gone prime time.

Chapter Eleven

Dakota took the cell phone Viviana handed him with shaking hands.

"It's from the prosecuting attorney," she said, "so I'm sure the facts are correct."

The message began to play.

"This is Nick Jefferson. I wanted you to hear this from me before you hear it on the news, Viviana. Harry Cortez was shot a few minutes ago as he was leaving a crime scene. He's in surgery now, but his condition is listed as critical.

"Nothing indicates the shooting was related to the Compton case, but on the off chance that it was, I'm going to request short-term witness protection for you and Briana until after the trial. Call me back as soon as you get this message."

Viviana dropped to the edge of the bed. "I

can't believe it. Why would someone try to kill Detective Cortez? I can't even see how that would help Hank's position."

"Cortez puts killers behind bars. That had to make him a few enemies along the way."

"I don't know which hospital he's in, but I can make a few calls and find out. Physicians have privileges when it comes to obtaining patient information."

"You need to call the attorney back, as well," Dakota said. "Does he know that you're in Mustang Run?"

"No, and frankly I'm surprised by his sudden concern about my safety. He never even calls me about the trial. I usually talk to his assistant."

"He wants that case to go to trial next week and he plans to make sure his number-one witness is there."

"No one wants that case to go to trial more than I do. Who knew just putting a guilty man behind bars could be this difficult?"

Troy would tell her it was easier to frame an innocent man. But Dakota understood Viviana's frustration and fear. He was feeling the heat of battle himself right now. He had to ask the question, though he dreaded her answer.

"Do you want to accept the attorney's offer of protection, Viviana?"

She looked up and met his gaze. "Do you want to get rid of me?"

"No. I want you and Briana right here with me. I can even tolerate staying at the ranch if it means keeping you both safer."

"Then why ask?"

Because his reasons for wanting her here weren't all noble. "I just want you to feel safe."

Viviana stood and fit herself against him, wrapping her hands around his waist. "I've never felt more safe in my life."

He held her close, feeling her heart beat against his chest, drinking in the flowery fragrance of her hair, remembering the taste of her lips on his.

He hated to let her go.

Briana had other ideas. Her high-pitched wails echoed down the long hallway.

Viviana slipped from his arms. "Nap time has officially ended."

She rushed off, leaving him to swallow the desire that was swelling inside him and go to

work on discovering who shot Dirty Harry.
He figured he'd start by harassing the SAPD
and by alerting his brothers that the heat had
been turned up a notch.

THREE OF THE FIVE Ledger brothers and their
father were present and accounted for in the
newly constructed ranch headquarters by
eight o'clock Saturday morning.

Headquarters consisted of two rooms, built
as an extension off the back of Dylan's house.
One was a small office with the usual business equipment and a functional desk.

The second room was a spacious area with
a rectangular metal table and an assortment
of mismatched chairs that looked as if they
had come from a used furniture store. Books
on cattle selection, maintaining cattle health,
growing your herd and countless other ranching topics half filled a large wooden book-
shelf.

A huge interactive map of the ranch covered most of one wall. Dylan had explained
its significance while they were waiting on
Sean to arrive. The map divided the ranch
into sections, each one labeled as *E, W, N* or
S followed by a number. Flagged pins denoted

which pastures held what percentage of the cattle at any given time.

The Willow Creek Ranch was a much more impressive operation than Dakota had anticipated. Under other circumstances, Dakota would have enjoyed hearing more about it. Today, though, his entire focus was on making sure that neither Hank Bateman nor any of his hit men set foot on the ranch.

If Hank was behind the attack on Harry Cortez, then his desperation level had just spilled over the top. Obviously he was willing to go to any length to stay out of prison.

As soon as the brotherly arm punches, back-whacking and hand-shaking were done, the men settled in chairs around the table and got down to the business at hand.

"I have bits and pieces of the situation," Sean said, "but I'd like to hear the full story."

Dakota recapped, leaving out nothing except the fact that being with Viviana and not really being with her was driving him crazy.

Sean scribbled a few notes on a pad he'd pulled from his shirt pocket. "So you just found out a few days ago that you're a father?"

"Yeah. Sounds strange, I know, but Viviana

and I had decided to end the relationship. She was doing her residency. I was on the road all the time."

"Dakota's personal life isn't up for debate," Troy said. "If Viviana and Briana were virtual strangers when they showed up on this ranch, we'd still feel duty bound to protect them."

"Point made," Sean said. "So where are Viviana and Briana now?"

"They're in the house visiting with Collette," Dakota replied, realizing he was grateful for the distraction that Dylan's wife provided Viviana.

"And you're sure she wants to turn down the offer of temporary protection from the authorities?" Dylan asked.

"She says she'd rather stay here on the ranch."

"Can't say I blame her." Dylan nodded and leaned back in his chair. "I took the liberty of talking to Collette's father last night. Glenn's been the sheriff in this county for decades. He says he can guarantee that if the government offered witness protection, they're convinced that Viviana and Briana are in imminent danger."

Dakota was well aware of Glenn McGuire's longevity and reputation. He'd been sheriff when Dakota's mother was murdered. In fact, he'd arrested Troy. If it bothered Troy to have Glenn McGuire brought into this, he didn't show it.

"What was McGuire's take on the situation?" Sean asked.

"He thinks we should hire Daniel Riker to set up a protection plan on the ranch with the primary emphasis being on watching the house where Viviana is staying."

"What kind of qualifications does Riker have?" Troy asked.

"He retired last year, but he was in special operations with the Dallas Police Department for the last ten years of his career. He was on the SWAT team in Garland before that. He's won countless titles in sharpshooting competitions with other law enforcement personnel."

"What about Trent Fontaine?" Sean asked.

Neither name registered with Dakota. "What's Trent's claim to fame?"

Troy rubbed the scar that trailed from his right cheek to his breastbone. "He's the retired Texas Ranger who's been helping me look for your mother's killer. I gave him a call last night, as well."

"He's a good man, too," Dylan said. "Did he have any suggestions?"

"He said pity the man who went up against the Ledgers."

"Damn straight," Dylan said. "Was that all Fontaine had to say?"

"He said watch each other's backs, expect the worst of anyone we don't know who tries to set foot on the ranch and if we had any questions, we could call him anytime."

"Was Trent interested in working protection at Willow Creek?" Sean asked.

"He's currently under contract to a private group along the border, trying to keep the illegal drug traffickers from killing the ranchers and their families and taking control of their land."

"That rules him out," Sean said.

"I'm willing to consider having a professional coordinate the protection efforts," Dakota said. "But when push comes to shove, I have the final say on everything."

"That goes without saying," Troy said. "Viviana's the mother of your child."

"We're pushing around ideas," Dylan said,

"but it's your call, Dakota. We can chase this horse in circles for another couple of hours or you can just tell us how you want us to help. We're behind you all the way."

"I appreciate that," Dakota said. "But I'd like to hear your opinions on hiring Riker or going it alone." He meant it and those were words he'd never expected to come out of his mouth.

He was a loner. He made friends, but he kept them at a distance, never sharing too much of himself, never wanting to know much about them. Never fully trusting anyone.

He'd come close with Viviana. That had cost him his heart and his chance to make the world finals last year.

But it had given him a daughter.

"My vote is that we keep this in the family and we take care of things ourselves," Dylan said. "If we need law enforcement to come and make an arrest, we go to the sheriff."

Dakota turned to Sean. "What about you?"

A hairy, black spider made the fatal mistake of crawling too close to Sean. He lifted his foot and squashed it beneath the heel of his boot.

"That's my decision." He lifted his foot and kicked the dead spider across the floor. "If that baby-murdering bully shows up here, we'll squash him the way I did that spider. I relish the chance. And I won't need an outsider to tell me how to do it."

They all looked to Troy, even Dakota. He didn't need his father, but Troy had spent years in prison. He had far more experience with the depraved factions of the human race than the rest of them put together.

"I'm with you, but never underestimate a desperate enemy. Most men will go to any lengths to avoid a life in prison, especially if they know the hell it really is."

Yet from what Dakota had heard from his uncle, Troy hadn't fought at all.

But then his uncle had a way of seeing whatever he chose in any situation.

"I'm with you," Dakota said, "except that I'd like to hire some off-duty cops to work under my command and keep a close watch on the house or any other place on the ranch where Viviana might choose to go. I'll want that 24/7. I'll pay all the expenses."

Sean nodded in agreement. "I can arrange for off-duty cops out of Austin if you want. I trained a couple of problem horses for their chief of police."

"Then I'll leave that up to you," Dakota said. "I'd like them on the job no later than tomorrow morning."

"I'll let you know if I run into any problems."

Within an hour the rules of operation had been established. Julie was to stay at Sean and Eve's for a few days. Collette was to have either Dylan or a couple of their most dependable wranglers with her at all times. Dakota wouldn't leave Viviana or Briana alone unless he'd notified Troy so that he could be available for any emergency.

That left Troy and Dylan free to run the ranch for most of the day, though they both wanted to be alerted by cell phone if any problems developed.

Dakota's brothers had come through for him. So had Troy. And yet Dakota still felt as if they were miles apart. The intervening years had taken too much of a toll on his ability to think of himself as part of a family. Closing the gap would be next to impossible.

"I'M GONNA BE A bull rider when I grow up, too, Uncle Dakota."

"It's not all fun. Those bulls can sure kick hard." Dakota looked down at the cute little towheaded nephew who'd been following him around ever since he arrived, staring up at him as if he were a superhero in jeans. This time he'd followed Dakota out the back door to take out the trash.

"I'm already practicing for the rodeo, but all Daddy will let me do so far is barrel riding for little kids."

"That's a good start. There's lots of coordination involved in getting that horse to do exactly what you want him to do. Plus, you learn to react to the animal's movements and mood."

"My daddy knows all about horses. He's a whisperer."

"I know. Now that takes real skill."

"He says the horses talk to him. They just don't use words. He says they talk to everybody, but some people just don't listen."

Sean joined them on the back porch. "Speaking of horses, why don't we take a walk to the horse barn and you can show

Uncle Dakota the two young colts that were born last month."

"The walk would do me good," Dakota said. He'd been cooped up in the house all afternoon and his injuries were tightening up on him. "Give me a minute to see if Viviana needs help with Briana."

He found Viviana in the dining room, spreading a large plaid tablecloth over a massive oak table. His daughter was nowhere in sight. "Where's Briana?"

"Meeting all her new aunts and being spoiled rotten. Collette has her at the moment. They're in the garden cutting a bouquet of fresh blossoms for the table."

An uneasy feeling ripped through him. "A grandfather. Aunts. Cousin Joey. You're rushing into this family concept awfully fast."

She smoothed the cloth. "You're Briana's father. This is your family. It's a package deal. Besides, I was an only child. I love the warmth and openness of family, especially this one."

"Don't get too comfortable with this."

"Don't worry. I have no expectations of home and hearth with you. The bulls would wreck the floors."

Now he'd irritated her. "Sean wants me to walk down to the horse barn with him."

"Great idea." She dismissed him with a toss of her head.

He rejoined Sean on the back porch and they started down the well-worn path to the horse barn. Dakota had no memories of the old one, but Dylan had mentioned that they'd doubled the size of it since he'd married Collette. She loved raising and training the animals and she'd learned a lot about both from Sean.

Joey ran ahead of them with his dog, Sparky, at his heels.

"Your stepson seems crazy about you," Dakota said. "He told me what a great whisperer you are."

"I can't seem to get away from the term *whisperer,* though I've tried. It makes me sound like I put some kind of magic spell on the animals. Believe me, I deal in common sense, not mumbo jumbo."

"Stick with *whisperer,*" Dakota teased. "It has a much better ring to it than commonsenser."

"Good thinking. And even whispering

is not quite as high on the hero list as bull riding."

"Less risk to the family jewels, though."

"There is that. Though I've had a wild stallion or two try to make a steer of me."

Dakota smiled. "You don't want that to happen, not with a woman like Eve to go home to every night."

"She is remarkable," Sean agreed. "I had no intention of ever saying 'I do.' And then I met Eve and suddenly that was all she wrote. I bit the dust with little more than a whimper."

"It sounds like you're a lucky man."

"Very lucky, which is not to say that Eve and I agree on everything. Not to change the subject, but what's the latest on Detective Cortez?"

"Viviana checked a couple of hours ago and his nurse reported that he's in and out of consciousness but still critical. It will be touch-and-go for the next twelve hours."

"Any word on who shot him?"

"Nothing official, and, apparently, he's too out of it to even remember getting shot. A detective named Gordon Miles is handling that investigation and also replacing Cortez in investigating the recent threat and attacks against Viviana."

"But the case is still on the trial docket?"

Dakota nodded. "Jury selection starts on Friday."

Joey reached the horse barn and disappeared inside. Loud neighing and some snorts welcomed his arrival.

"Joey loves horses, and he's a natural in the saddle," Sean said.

"I get that part of the family picture," Dakota said. "It's the way you all rally around Troy I find hard to buy. Even if he didn't kill Mother, he didn't give a damn what happened to us and you know it."

The anger erupted before Dakota could stop it, but he wasn't really sorry he'd said how he felt.

"He tried to get in touch with us. Our grandparents got a court order to stop him. They even went so far as to falsify a letter from Wyatt telling him that none of us wanted to hear from him."

"All I know is that I was six years old and nobody cared what happened to me."

"How can you say that? You were the only one of us who got to go home with Grandma."

"Who immediately went into a deep depression."

"We only heard she was sick at the time. But then you got to go and live in Montana with Uncle Larry."

"Yeah, good old Uncle Larry." Sarcasm cut through his voice.

"Guess that didn't go so well, either, huh?"

"Hardly."

"No one knew that," Sean said.

"No one bothered to find out."

"I'm sorry."

"Not your fault. Just don't expect me to suddenly start thinking of Troy as this great father figure of the Ledger clan."

"No one's selling that story, Dakota. Dad's not a saint. He's just a man. But he loved Mom. And he's doing what he can now. I guess that's good enough for me."

"I may have missed the forgiveness gene."

"Give yourself time. Viviana and fatherhood may change your way of thinking about a lot of things."

"You do know that Viviana and I aren't really together."

"Aren't you? She trusts you enough that she's here with you instead of in a safe house.

You're here protecting her and Briana instead of chasing another world championship buckle."

"That's all temporary."

"All I'm saying is, don't go yanking the saddle off the bucking horse before you've done all you can to ride."

"Advice from a whisperer?"

"Common sense from a brother."

Joey stuck his head out from the barn. "Are you guys coming?"

"Yep. I was just telling your uncle what a great little horseman you are." Sean threw his arm around Dakota's shoulder and lowered his voice. "Don't be so hard on Troy or yourself. You're a Ledger. You'll do what's right for Viviana and Briana."

To Dakota's way of thinking, being a Ledger had never been a plus. He had little faith in that changing anytime soon, if ever.

VIVIANA JOINED EVE and Julie on the wide front porch. "Briana is already sleeping soundly. I think all the activity wore her out."

"She's so adorable," Julie said. "I can't wait for Tyler to return from Afghanistan so that we can start a family."

Viviana settled on the top step next to Julie. "When will he be discharged?"

"He has nine more months of active service, but he may return to the States before that. That's the day I'll truly start celebrating."

And between now and then Julie must be living in fear that Tyler might be killed or maimed while fighting for his country, Viviana thought. She had to wake to that possibility every day and go to bed with that apprehension hanging over her every night. Yet, her blue eyes danced with excitement when she talked about him.

Collette pushed through the front door carrying a tray. "Dessert," she announced. "Cookies, compliments of Eve. The citrus slush is my concoction. All healthy and cooling."

Eve's brows arched. "Is the evening too hot for your usual coffee?"

"I'm trying to cut down on my caffeine, but there's coffee brewing in the kitchen if you'd rather have it."

"No, I'm fine with half-frozen lemonade," Eve assured her. She stood and helped pass out the drinks and the cookies before she and Collette both settled onto the porch swing.

Viviana was amazed by the way the three sisters-in-law got along, especially when they were all so different in looks and personalities.

Dylan's wife Collette was friendly, yet cautious. She seemed to fit into ranch life as if it were a second skin, especially when she talked of the horses. Yet she looked like a confident model tonight with her thick red curls tumbling over her beautiful bare shoulders and the white sundress dancing about her knees.

Eve was quieter, soft-spoken, insightful. At least that was Viviana's first impression of her. Her brown hair was cut into a sensible bob that fell to her chin. She clearly adored Sean and had a warm and loving relationship with Joey.

Julie was a vivacious blonde. Full of energy. Quick to laugh. Madly in love with her soldier husband.

"Isn't it great when the men offer to do cleanup?" Collette commented. "It gives us a chance to gossip."

"Speaking of which, what happened with

Troy's housekeeper?" Eve asked. "All I heard was how wonderfully she was working out and the next thing I hear she's quit."

"It's the haunted-house rumor," Julie said. "Some woman in town told her how she'd seen a woman in white standing in the window one night and it scared the wits out of her."

"That story's been circulating ever since Helene's murder," Eve said. "You'd think it would die down now that people are living in the house again."

Fortunately, Viviana did not believe in ghosts.

Julie wrapped her hands around her legs and leaned against the post at the top of the steps. "On the more notorious gossip front, Troy's former neighbor, Senator Foley, made the news again."

"Not another conquest?"

"Yes, and as usual, the love interest is married and half his age."

"Have any of you ever met the senator?" Eve asked.

"I've met him several times," Collette said. "I've been one of his constituents for years."

"What's he like?"

"He's charismatic, but not particularly handsome."

"I think his ex-wife is after Troy," Eve said.

"I agree," Julie said. "You should see the blouse she wore over here last week. It left little to the imagination. But I'm not sure I blame her. She is very attractive, and Troy would be a great catch if it weren't for the fact that he's obsessed with finding Helene's killer."

"For some reason, Sean doesn't like Ruthanne Foley," Eve said. "He never says why, but I can tell he doesn't like it when Troy mentions that she's stopped by."

"Enough about Ruthanne Foley," Julie said. "Viviana is going to think we're a bunch of catty snobs."

"No way," she assured them.

Actually she knew that they were intentionally trying to keep her mind off her own situation and she appreciated their efforts. It didn't work, of course. How could it, when even now Dakota and his brothers were likely talking about Hank Bateman and speculating as to what heinous act he'd resort to next?

The women jumped from one topic to another over the next half hour, starting with

Eve's volunteer work with an agency dedicated to finding adoptive parents for handicapped youngsters and finally getting to Collette's announcement that she and Dylan were planning to start a new wing on their house.

"You just added an office wing for ranch headquarters," Eve noted. "Aren't you tired of all that construction?"

"No. I like the idea of more room."

"For the two of you?"

"We won't always be just two."

Julie jumped up from the step and walked over to stand next to the swing. "You're pregnant, aren't you?"

Collette rubbed her hand over her belly. "Do I look pregnant?"

"Yes. You're glowing," Julie said. "Besides a new wing, a sudden need to cut down on caffeine. You may as well wear a sign."

Collette flashed a conspiratorial smile. "Okay, since you dragged it out of me. I'm pregnant."

Julie squealed as she tugged Collette from the swing and into a bear hug. "I'm so happy for you."

"Does Dylan know?" Eve asked as she threw her arms around Collette.

"He does. He's deliriously excited. We were going to tell all of you this weekend at dinner, but then he thought we should wait until the threat of danger to Viviana and Briana is past. But I couldn't hold it in another second."

"I've disrupted all your lives," Viviana said, walking over to join them. "I guess I was selfish in not thinking—"

"Nonsense." Collette pulled her into a hug and interrupted her apology. "We all came into the Ledger family the same way. I'm beginning to think that the only way you can win a Ledger's heart is by needing his protection."

"It's that cowboy-code thing," Julie said. "They're all a bunch of heroes just waiting to be needed before their passion can be unleashed."

That hadn't been the case with Dakota. With him, the passion had been explosive from day one. Then came fatherhood. And then danger. Love and commitment showed no sign of emerging.

"Dakota is definitely protective," she said and left it at that.

The chatter and easy camaraderie continued until Sean joined them and said it was time to go. Julie left with them. She was spending a few days with Eve and Sean at their horse farm in Bandera.

"You're very quiet," Collette said to Viviana once the others had left. "Is there anything you'd like to talk about?"

"No, I'm just tired. The last few days have been trying and exhausting."

"I'm sure. We didn't get to you with that talk of the house being haunted, did we?"

"No. I don't believe in ghosts or spirits."

"Even if you did, there's nothing to fear. Helene's spirit might be intrusive and a bit creepy at times, but it's not dangerous."

The comment surprised Viviana. Collette seemed so levelheaded. "Are you telling me that you believe Helene's ghost still haunts this house?"

"No. Pay no attention to me. It's just that sometimes I have a very active imagination."

Viviana had enough real trouble in her life without looking for spirits or letting her imagination run wild. She said good-night and went inside. Dylan, Troy and Dakota were still talking in the kitchen, but she didn't disturb them to say good-night. For once her thoughts weren't all centered on the upcoming trial and Hank Bateman.

It was Helene Ledger's murder that stalked her mind as she walked down the long, dimly lit hallway to the guestroom, the room directly across from the master suite that Helene had shared with Troy Ledger so many years ago.

VIVIANA WAS TUBING down the Guadalupe River, the swiftly flowing water carrying her faster and faster, rushing past people on the banks frantically waving and yelling for her to get out of the river.

The water that had been warm at first grew colder and colder until the chill seeped into her bones.…

Viviana jerked awake and reached for the quilt she'd kicked to the foot of the bed. Only remnants of the nightmare remained but a cold draft swept across her shivering body. Even if a door was open, it couldn't be this cold unless someone had turned the air conditioner on full blast.

She should check on Briana. But when she tried to push to a sitting position, it was as if her shoulders were pinned to the bed.

And then a voice, low and broken, echoed about the dark room.

"I had a baby once, too."

Chapter Twelve

White ribbons flashed across the room like lightning.

Viviana's heart pounded in her chest so loudly that it echoed about the room.

"You should be very afraid."

"Who are you?" Viviana asked.

"A mother. Babies need their mother."

"Is that you, Helene?"

The ribbons flashed again and then coalesced into a woman's shape that hovered over Viviana's head.

"No one took care of my baby. No one protected him."

"Your baby is Dakota. He's a man, Helene. He's here. He's come home."

"No." The figure disintegrated. When it did the ribbons turned red and cracked like whips above the bed. "Dakota is lost. Find him, Viviana. Find him and bring him home."

"He is home, Helene. He's in the same room where he used to sleep."

"No. He's lost in Montana. Wounded. Afraid. You and Briana must save him."

"Briana's just a baby, Helene. Dakota is strong and protective. He's saving us."

"Hold on tight to Dakota. If you let go of him, he will be lost forever."

The words made no sense. And the room grew colder, still. Viviana could feel bands of ice forming around her heart. "Did Troy kill you, Helene? Is that why you can't let go?"

Balls of fire darted across the room, dispelling the chill.

"Did Troy shoot you, Helene? Tell me and I can make him pay."

"Love doesn't kill. But it can destroy. Don't destroy my son."

A searing heat shot through Viviana as if one of the balls of fire had cut right through her flesh. The ribbons cracked one last time and then they were gone.

Only the heat remained. For a second, Viviana thought the whole house must surely be on fire. She jumped from the bed. The second her feet touched the floor, the heat dissipated.

The temperature cooled to normal in a heartbeat. Viviana's heart found a steady rhythm.

A nightmare. That's all it had been. It had seemed incredibly real, but it was just a stupid nightmare induced by the evening's talk of ghosts, spirits and haunted happenings.

Viviana's cotton nightshirt was damp and sticking to her like syrup. She yanked it open and let it drop to the floor while she reached for the robe she'd left hanging on one of the posts of the antique bed.

Once it was cinched, she stooped to pick up the nightshirt so that she could toss it out of the way. A wide strand of white ribbon clung to the collar.

A shudder ripped through Viviana.

Hold on tight to Dakota. If you let go of him, he will be lost forever.

Only how could Viviana hold on to him if he didn't want to be held?

She tiptoed from the room and stepped across the hall to check on Briana. Her heart jumped to her throat when she saw the shadowy figure standing by the bed.

"I thought I heard Briana cry out, but she's fast asleep."

Dakota. Only Dakota. She took a deep

breath and let the air fill her lungs before slowly exhaling.

"I didn't hear her," Viviana said. "I just woke and came to check on her."

"Does she always sleep with her little rump stuck up like that?" Dakota asked.

"Usually."

They stood silently, side by side, staring at the child that seemed to hold them together at the same time she pushed them apart.

"Did you hate me when you found out you were pregnant?" Dakota whispered.

"I've never hated you, Dakota."

"You chose not to have me in your life."

"I didn't want to love you when you were never going to be mine."

"I was yours."

"For a week. But you'd made it clear from the first day we met that you were addicted to bull riding and to..."

"Never sleeping too many nights in the same place," he whispered, finishing the statement for her. "That was the code I've lived by since I ran away from home at sixteen."

He reached into the crib and let his fingers entwine with the soft locks of Briana's dark, curly hair. "You were right to send me away. I have nothing to offer. I wouldn't be good for you or Briana."

Hold on tight to Dakota. If you let go of him, he will be lost forever.

"I think you have a lot more to offer than you realize. We could start over, Dakota, this time as friends and see where it goes from there."

"I'm not sure I could stop at just being friends." He bent closer to her, so close she felt his breath on her skin, so close she could almost taste his lips.

Her knees grew weak. Any claim to control vanished, and she closed her eyes in anticipation.

The kiss never came.

When she opened her eyes, Dakota was staring at the display on his cell phone.

"Good that I had it on vibrate," he whispered. "I'm sorry, but I have to take this call."

"Go right ahead."

She followed him into the hallway and watched as he retreated to his room. She wondered if there had really been a call or if he'd just needed an escape.

Not that it mattered, she told herself.

There had been no ghostly vision and Dakota wasn't lost. He was exactly what he wanted to be. Sexy as hell. Brave enough to take on anything…except commitment.

BRIANA MADE UP for going to sleep early by waking at six. Viviana dragged herself from bed, pulled on her robe and went to get Briana before she woke Troy and Dakota. Troy needed his rest and Viviana had no interest in talking to Dakota after the way he'd wormed his way out of the kiss.

"Good morning, sweet angel. You slept well last night. I think ranch living agrees with you. Or do you just like having Momma here instead of Claire when you wake up?"

Briana kicked her feet and legs, then rolled over and got up on her hands and knees as if trying to help Viviana get her out of bed.

"First we'd best get rid of that wet diaper. Then we'll go find breakfast."

Briana cooed and uttered a string of baby gibberish, bouquets of sounds that Viviana always hoped would come out as *Momma*. It hadn't happened yet, but Viviana knew it would come any day now.

The neckline of Briana's pajamas was wet,

as well. Cutting teeth were accompanied by excessive drooling. Viviana slipped a cute polka-dot knit top over Briana's dry diaper.

"Now you're ready to enchant the world."

Troy was sitting at the kitchen table sipping coffee and poring over the morning paper when she and Briana entered. "You're up early," he said.

"I could say the same for you."

"Rancher's hours."

"It's Sunday."

"The cows don't know that. But actually Dakota got me up even earlier than usual this morning."

"Don't tell me he's ranching?"

"No. He left for San Antonio about thirty minutes ago. Didn't he tell you?"

"No." Apprehension settled in the pit of her stomach. Briana began to squirm and she switched her to the other hip. "Why is he going to San Antonio?"

"He said he had a call from one of his bull-rider friends and he needed to go and help him with a problem."

Maybe that had been a legitimate call he'd gotten in Briana's room last night. But what could a bull-riding friend want that was so important that Dakota had to drive to San Antonio at daybreak?

Surely Dakota hadn't just decided to dump her and Briana on his family while he reentered the competition.

"Da pa ba a da."

Viviana frowned. *You better not even think of muttering "Dada" before you say "Mama." I'll sell you to the highest bidder.* She took Briana's plastic cereal bowl and coated baby spoon from the bottom shelf of the cabinet.

Troy stood, walked to the counter and held out his hands to Briana. "Why don't you come to Grandpa while your mother gets your breakfast ready?"

To Viviana's surprise, Briana went right to him.

She poured the cereal into the bowl and then took a jar of pureed applesauce from the refrigerator. "Did Dakota happen to mention which friend he was going to see?"

"No, he just wanted to make sure I would be here to keep a close watch on you and Briana."

Troy stayed to visit while she fed Briana.

"I don't know if this is the best time to go into this, but I had a call from my son Wyatt last night after both you and Dakota had gone to bed. He was able to find out quite a bit about the George Bateman who was in prison with me."

"Like what?"

"For starters, he is the brother of the Hank Bateman accused of killing Leslie Compton."

"So we know criminal behavior runs in the family. What else did Wyatt discover about the Batemans?"

"George was in prison with me. He'd been convicted of armed robbery of a small mom-and-pop grocery store. But robbery wasn't enough for George. He tied up the couple who owned the place, tormented and tortured them for hours and finally shot both of them in the stomach. Then he set fire to the building and left them alive to burn to death."

"How sick and depraved. Two murders should have earned him at least life in prison. How is it that he's already a free man?"

"The couple escaped and survived so he was tried on a lesser charge than murder one. He was sentenced to twenty years and served ten. It's how the system works."

"If fire is George's weapon of choice, then it's not surprising that Hank would have my car set on fire. He's learned from the best of the worst. He might have even had George do that bit of depravity for him." She shook her head, as if to erase the image.

"Does Dakóta know any of this?"

"He knows all of it. I relayed it to him just as he was leaving for San Antonio. Now tell me more about the death of that infant," Troy said.

"Hank Bateman brought the child into the E.R. about one in the morning."

"Where was the mother?"

"Working. She was a prostitute. Hank didn't tell us that, but Cortez discovered her profession in his investigation. She'd been arrested several times."

"Was the baby still alive when Hank showed up at the emergency room?"

"Alive, but unconscious. Hank claimed she'd rolled onto the floor from a bed where she'd been sleeping. I knew from the excessive retinal hemorrhaging and the pattern of bruising that he was lying. I notified the police department and they assigned Harry Cortez to the case. The autopsy findings bore out my claims of nonaccidental trauma to the brain."

"How did Hank react that night?"

"He was nervous. He even seemed a little panicked—more for himself than the child."

"But it was his kid?"

"Yes. DNA testing has proved that Leslie Compton was his biological child, but he and the mother were not married."

"Are they still together?"

"No."

"Will the mother testify against him?"

"That was the original plan, but now Karen Compton's disappeared. The prosecutor believes she's off on a drug binge."

"I'd say it's more likely Hank got to her."

"You think he abducted her?"

"It's possible. That might have been what the gunman in the E.R. parking lot had planned for you."

"He would have likely been successful if Dakota hadn't shown up when he did."

"Dakota's a good man, Viviana. I know things aren't right between the two of you, but he'll be a good father to Briana. He just needs time to adjust to the idea of fatherhood."

"I'm sorry now that I didn't find a way to contact him when Briana was born."

"We all have regrets, Viviana. Don't waste

time worrying about what might have been or what could have been. Take the advice of a man who lost almost two decades of his life. Time is much too precious to waste."

Was that what she was doing? Losing the present? Destroying the future?

Hold on tight to Dakota.

Had that been her own good sense speaking, trying to break through to her consciousness any way it could?

DAKOTA STOOD AT THE DOOR to Jim Angle's hotel room, his temper exploding as he plunged into a state of absolute fury. "Why didn't you tell me they'd beat the hell out of you when you called last night?"

"Because all they'd done then was make a phone call and demand I tell them where you and Viviana had gone." Jim dabbed at the blood spilling from the space where a front tooth used to be. "They made personal contact this morning to finish making their point."

"When were they here?"

"You missed them by about ten minutes. If you'd driven a little faster we could have made it a real party."

"I don't suppose you caught their names?"

"Nope, but one of them has a killer right punch."

"What did they look like?"

"Two thugs in ski masks."

"Any identifying marks? Tattoos? Scars? Blemishes?"

"One of them has a black eye. I got in one good left hook before I went down. But the guy who did the punching was the same one who made all the threats on the phone last night. I recognized his voice. The bastard who did the holding didn't say much."

"Exactly what was their message?"

"The same as I told you last night. If I liked waking up mornings I'd best tell them where you and Viviana had gone."

"Did you tell them?"

"Do I look like a damned traitor?"

"You look like you just got run over by a cement truck."

"Either that or by Devil's Deed on steroids. You look like you're recovering, though."

"I'm well enough to take care of the men who did this to you."

"That's not your job."

"Says who?"

Dakota pulled out his cell phone and made a call to Detective Gordon Miles. He got nothing from him except the assurance that Hank Bateman was not at his brother's apartment. If he was, they would have found and arrested him by now. It had been the first place they'd looked for Hank when he'd slipped his tail.

Dakota's next call was to his brother Wyatt.

"It's Sunday. I'm off duty. Take two aspirin and call me in the morning."

"Sorry, bro. I've got an emergency."

"Dakota. It's you. What's up?"

"I need an address for George Bateman. Can you get that for me?"

"I gave it to Dad a few minutes ago. You two should try conversing."

"I'm not at the ranch, but he did give me the rest of the scoop on George Bateman before I left."

"Okay. Hold on a minute."

Dakota held for two.

"Sorry," Wyatt said when he got back to the phone. "The street number was buried in one of the files. But I found it."

Dakota scribbled George Bateman's address on the hotel notepad when Wyatt repeated it.

"Tell me you're not going to do anything stupid like go visit George Bateman without backup."

"I'd never tell you that."

"Putting our lives on the line is why we cops make the big bucks. Call them."

"I tried that. They're uncooperative."

"Then take friends or family."

"I'm taking two friends. Smith and Wesson. And I'm just going to have a little chat."

"Stay alive, Dakota. It's the best way to make the criminals really mad. Plus dead heroes never get the woman."

"I'll make a note of that."

Jim had pulled off his bloody shirt while Dakota was talking to Wyatt and was trying to shrug his arms into a clean one. "If you're going to see George Bateman, I'm going with you."

"As the poster child for the importance of avoiding bullies?"

"As your backup."

"Fine. Let's go. My truck is waiting."

GEORGE BATEMAN stood at the front window, watching as Dakota Ledger climbed from his fancy new pickup truck. The dope was really making this convenient.

George pulled his gun and aimed it at Dakota's head. He could put the bullet right between the cowboy's eyes. Seeing him dead would be a kick but getting rid of the body would be the really fun part.

He'd deliver it to Dr. Mancini and leave it in her bed. What a homecoming present that would be. And next time somebody told the bitch to mind her own business, she might pay attention.

One step inside the door and then George would have to shoot the trespasser. In fear for his life. Even if he got caught, no judge could argue with that.

He didn't plan to get caught. He was much too smart to let that happen again. Murder and payback had become a cottage industry for him.

Chapter Thirteen

Dakota had made three stops on the way to the home of George Bateman. The first was to the E.R., where he had forcefully dragged Jim out of the truck and left him yelling curses a few feet from the front entrance.

The second stop was to a Walmart, where he'd purchased a lightweight windbreaker. The third had been to pawn shop that was open on Sundays, where he picked up a shoulder holster that fit over his lucky red shirt and beneath the light windbreaker that was already causing him to sweat profusely.

George's apartment was on the first floor, right side, of a fourplex. The windows of the left side had been boarded over and the building looked as if it had recently been gutted by fire. He wondered if the tenants had gotten on George's bad side.

It was twenty minutes before ten and the streets were deserted except for two kids who looked to be about ten years old. They were riding their bikes down the middle of the street and popping wheelies. Dakota would have to make sure the boys weren't hit by stray bullets if his chat with George turned into all-out war.

Hank might not be around, but someone was home at the Bateman residence. Dakota had seen the blinds shift slightly in the front window when he'd driven up.

He rang the bell and waited. Shelby Lucas came to the door. He hadn't been expecting her. Her face was swollen, her right eye circled in purplish bruises.

She looked to her left as if waiting for a signal. "Come in," she mumbled and stepped aside.

Dakota smelled the trap as surely as if it had been set with Roquefort cheese. He pulled his gun. George's was already pointed at his head. Neither backed off.

George smirked. "Had I known there was going to be a duel, I would have dressed for the occasion."

"Had Jim Angle known he was going to be

jumped by a couple of worthless thugs, he'd have given you a better fight."

"Sorry, Dakota Ledger, but I don't know a Jim Angle."

"I don't suppose you know Dr. Viviana Mancini, either."

"I've heard of her. She's the bitch who's trying to frame my brother for murder when none was committed."

"A jury will decide that. Five days from now, George. There *will* be a trial. Dr. Mancini *will* testify."

"*Dr. Mancini.* That's rather formal for a woman you're sleeping with. You bull riders amaze me. You reek of bull dung while putting on airs."

"And we have extremely itchy fingers when they're resting on triggers."

"Just say what you have to say, Ledger. You're starting to bore me."

"Hank needs to turn himself in so that this trial can take place as scheduled."

"You're talking to the wrong person, Dakota. I'm not my brother's keeper."

"Then let me put it another way. If that trial doesn't start as scheduled, I'm going to hold you personally responsible. And if Hank or anyone else harms Dr. Mancini or her daughter, they *won't* live to regret it."

"Is that it, Ledger?"

"For now." Dakota started to back from the room when he saw the clench of George's jaw and the flick of his wrist. Dakota fired first, shooting the pistol from George's hand.

Shelby screamed.

George let out a stream of curses and grabbed his bleeding hand. "Get out of my house, you son of a murdering wife killer."

Dakota kicked George's gun beneath the couch. "Leave my dad out of this."

"Why should I, you pious fool? Troy bragged to everyone in prison that he'd killed your mother. She was a no-good tramp who was about to leave him for another man. He wasn't about to let her get away with that."

Rage consumed Dakota. He ached to pull the trigger again. He wanted so badly to kill George Bateman that his finger shook on the trigger.

One pull and he could blow the bastard into tiny pieces. He took a deep breath, then forced himself to switch the pistol to his right hand. He punched George as hard as he could.

His fist connected with Bateman's jaw with enough force to knock him against the wall.

George staggered for a second and then came back swinging. He caught Dakota in his bruised chest with a left jab. The pain was so intense Dakota couldn't breathe for long suffocating seconds.

George took advantage of the moment and wrestled the gun from Dakota's hand. It went off in the process and the bullet ricocheted about the room.

The next bullet hit the wall just past George's head, but that bullet had not come from Dakota's gun.

They both turned and stared at Shelby. She was standing just out of George's reach, his own gun aimed at his right temple. Somehow she'd retrieved it without either of them noticing.

"Drop the gun, George," Shelby said. "There's too much killing. Too much."

"Stay out of this, Shelby."

"No. Drop the gun before I count to five or I swear I'll kill you."

"You don't have the guts."

"One. Two."

Dakota looked Shelby square in the eye

and the cold, hard glaze convinced him that the timid and fearful woman had finally been pushed over the edge.

"Three."

"Put the gun down, Shelby," George ordered. "You'll never shoot me and you know it."

"Four."

George lunged at Shelby and she pulled the trigger. The bullet missed his chest by inches, digging into the muscle of his forearm. It was far from a fatal injury but it was enough that he dropped the gun and bolted for the door.

Shelby collapsed into a ball, crying as she rubbed her stomach.

Dakota started after George, but changed his mind. He'd said what he'd come to say. If he went after Bateman now and killed him, it would be cold-blooded murder.

With full malice intent. The same way Troy had killed Dakota's mother.

Dakota would never leave that legacy to Briana.

He holstered his gun and then knelt beside Shelby. She was still rubbing her stomach and crying.

"It's okay, Shelby. You shot George to keep

him from killing me and maybe even you. You can't go to prison for that. Even Hank will understand."

"Hank killed Leslie Compton." Her voice was shaky and hoarse. "I lied before when I said he didn't. I was trying to save him. Now he won't have anything to do with me. That's the thanks I get."

"Were you there when Hank killed the baby?" Dakota asked. "Can you testify as an eyewitness?"

"I wasn't there, but Hank told me he did it. The baby wouldn't stop crying so he started to shake her. And then something just came over him and he shook her until she went limp."

Dakota put an arm around her shaking shoulder. "You can't keep protecting him, Shelby."

"I know."

"You have to tell the police what Hank told you about killing Leslie Compton."

"The police won't believe anything I have to say."

"A jury might."

Dakota put in another call to Detective Gordon Miles. "I think you may want to meet me at George Bateman's apartment. I may have another witness for you in the Leslie Compton case."

WHEN DAKOTA hadn't returned by noon, Viviana was seriously apprehensive. He'd been at her side almost constantly since coming to her rescue in the parking lot. So what had happened to cause him to leave for hours without telling her where he was going and why?

She stretched out next to Briana's quilt, but even Briana's antics and babbling couldn't take her mind off Dakota.

Her pulse quickened when she heard a vehicle pull up and stop in the driveway. She picked up Briana and raced to the door. It was only Collette and Dylan with their hands full of covered bowls and pans with their handles cradled in hot pads.

"We brought lunch," Collette said.

"Enough for a week," Troy said, walking up behind Viviana.

"Or for three hungry men," Collette corrected.

"Right now there are only two hungry males," Troy said.

"Where's Dakota?" Collette asked after she said hello to Viviana and gave Briana a kiss.

"He went into San Antonio on business," Troy said.

Dylan's eyes reflected the concern that Viviana was feeling. "What kind of business?"

"He didn't say, but I got the idea it was urgent."

"Then he should have said where he was going and had one of us go with him. Either we're in this together or we're not. How long has he been gone?"

"Going on six hours now."

They started back to the kitchen with the food. "Dakota's not used to family," Troy said. "Cut him some slack. It takes a while to learn to trust. You remember how things were between you and me when I was first released from prison."

"This is different. Dakota should have called."

"He hasn't had to check in with me since he was six," Troy said. "I reckon he doesn't figure he has to start now."

Viviana placed Briana in her jump chair so that she could help serve the home-cooked meal of baked macaroni and cheese, salad and fried chicken. She was just about to sit down to her plate of food when the front door creaked open.

She stepped to the kitchen doorway in time to see Dakota turn the corner to the back of the house without even a glance toward the kitchen.

"It's Dakota," she announced to the others. "Collette, would you mind watching Briana for a few minutes?"

"Of course, I'll watch her. But don't be gone too long. The macaroni will get cold."

"No, I'll just be a minute or two."

Dakota tossed a pistol to the bed just as Viviana stepped into the room. Her apprehension became tangible. "Where have you been?"

"Taking care of business."

"With a gun?"

"As a matter of fact, that's exactly how I took care of it. But strike that panicked expression from your face. I haven't killed anyone. Yet."

She dropped to the side of the bed. "If this has anything to do with me or the trial, I have a right to know."

"You have a right to know a lot of things. And it's time that they were said."

VIVIANA SAT DUMBSTRUCK as she listened to Dakota's account of his morning's adventure. He'd taken on a hardened criminal all by himself, stood there with a gun pointed at him by a man who'd have had no qualms about killing him. Yet Dakota hadn't backed down.

He was fearless. Brave and courageous. A protector who didn't just wait for trouble to appear but went after it at its source.

She started to shake. "You could have been killed."

"I could have sat back and done nothing while the Brothers Gruesome beat up my friends and planned a way to keep you from testifying in court. I may not have accomplished much, but at least I let them know that I don't plan to roll over and play dead while they run over you."

"You did a lot, Dakota. You stood up for your friend. You stood up for me and you gave Shelby Lucas the courage to stand up for herself against the father of her unborn child."

"I think Hank did that when he proved to her what a perverted jerk he really was."

"But she might never have had the courage to act if you hadn't shot the gun from George's hand first. You let her know that neither he nor Hank were invincible."

"There you go making me into a hero when I'm just doing what needed to be done."

She fought tears and a surge of passion that triggered a myriad of mixed emotions. She stood and pressed her body against his, wrapping her arms around his neck. "You are a hero, Dakota."

She touched her lips to his and this time he didn't worm his way out of the kiss.

He took her mouth hungrily and she exploded with a need that rocked clear through to her soul. The kiss intensified and she reveled in every sensation it created. Her breath mingling with his. His tongue pushing its way into her mouth. The salty sweet taste of his lips. The hard, wanton heat of his need for her swelling between them.

His fingers tangled in her hair and then slid down her spine, pressing and kneading until they slipped inside the waistband of her white shorts and worked their way inside her panties.

He pressed her against his erection. Her heart beat so fast and so strong it felt as if it might burst from her body.

It was the middle of the day in his father's house, but Viviana could no more hold back the driving need inside her than she could stop time or reverse the spin of the earth. She yanked her shirt over her head and wiggled out of her bra so that her breasts were free.

Dakota cupped her breasts with his hands and gingerly sucked and nibbled the right nipple until it was rock hard and perfectly erect.

She felt the hot rush building inside her core.

"Take me, Dakota. All of me. I've waited for this for so long. Waited even when I told myself I didn't need you to make me complete."

Dakota pulled away as if her words had been thorns…or a trap.

"I can't do this, Viviana. Oh, God, I want you so badly, but I can't do this to you."

His rejection ripped at her heart like a jagged knife. "You can put your life on the line for me, but you can't make love with me. Are you that afraid you might actually find out that you need me?"

He shook his head and raked his fingers through his hair. "It's not that. It's nothing like that."

"Then what is it, Dakota? Talk straight like you claim you always do because I can't begin to figure out what you want from me. I thought it was sex without strings. But then I throw that at you and you turn it down."

"I'm Troy Ledger's son, Viviana."

"If that's your excuse, I'm not buying. Dylan and Tyler and Sean are Troy's sons and they lead perfectly normal lives. They may face a few negative comments from time to time, but they're man enough to take it. I'm sure you are, too."

"They're not Troy's sons the way I am. I wanted to kill George Bateman today. Not in self-defense. In rage. When he called my mother a tramp and said Troy bragged all over prison about how he'd murdered her, it was all I could do not to pull that trigger."

"But you didn't pull it, Dakota. You drew from something deep inside you and punched him instead."

"But one day I might not. I might give in to the rage just as Troy did. He must have tried to stop himself, yet when he flew into the rage, he pulled the trigger three times and left my mother lying in a pool of blood."

"You don't know that. Just because a lying, scumbag brute said it, that doesn't make it true."

"Why else would Troy have turned his back on us unless he knew he'd killed our mother, unless he knew that he had no more to offer us than I have to offer Briana?"

"So that will be your justification for turning your back on Briana? Some crazy notion that you have murderous tendencies in your DNA?"

She pulled on her clothes, hating that she'd bared her body and soul to him. "I thought you were brave, Dakota. I thought facing a killer for us demonstrated your courage. But that was the easy way out for you. It's like riding bulls. You relish the risks, as long as you don't ever have to put your emotions on the line."

"My emotions are on the line. They have been since the day I met you."

"Then be a real man, Dakota. Talk to

you father one-on-one and then put the past behind you. Do it for you. Do it for Briana. Do it for us."

Hold on tight to Dakota. If you let go of him, he will be lost forever.

She was trying, but Dakota was slipping from her grip.

Chapter Fourteen

Hank Bateman was sick of covering for his brother. George always had to be the tough guy. He started trouble everywhere he went.

But it was never knowing when to keep his mouth shut that was bringing them both down. Hank had a couple of small details to take care of and then he was cutting out and leaving George behind.

There were still a couple of kinks to work out but nothing he couldn't handle. He already had a map with the back roads to Willow Creek Ranch.

He knew he'd find Dr. Mancini there, thanks to the notes he'd lifted from Detective Cortez's notebook. The other reason was far more pressing. They were closing in on him and George. Time was running out.

A few more days and his new life would

start. Him and Karen, finally together. She needed him the way no other woman ever had. The authorities would search for them in Mexico, but they would never find them.

His flights to Switzerland were already bought and paid for. The fake IDs were almost ready.

The only task left was to kill the good doctor. Slow and painful. The kind of murder he'd always liked best.

Chapter Fifteen

Dakota spent the next hour sitting in the shade of a tree, whittling a broken limb with his pocketknife. He used to whittle a lot back in Montana.

There was never a pattern to his cuts. There was no skill involved. It was just watching the knife slit into the wood and seeing the chunks fall to the ground that tended to clear his mind when his thoughts became so muddled he couldn't think straight.

It might have all begun with Wyatt's knife and the niche Dakota had carved into the old dresser. He wondered how much of what he'd learned in those early years on the ranch were part of the man he was now even though he didn't remember most of that time.

The chunks were flying fast and furious today, but the muddle refused to clear. Maybe

Viviana was right. He needed to level with his father.

There were things that needed to be said. Hurtful things. Painful truths. Difficult questions that had tormented Dakota since he was six years old.

He found Troy in the workshop, making what looked to be a rocking horse from knotty pine.

Dakota leaned against the carpenter's bench. "Have you got a minute?"

"I've got all the time you need."

Troy laid down the plane he'd been using to smooth the horse's wooden mane. "I guess this talk has been a long time in coming."

Dakota brushed some sawdust from the edge of the table. "About nineteen years."

"Ask whatever you want."

"Tell me how you met Mother?"

"That's an easy one. I was working as a wrangler at the Black Spur Ranch to earn money for my rodeo fees. I was a bull rider, same as you, only not nearly as good.

"I wasn't from Mustang Run but I'd become good friends with Sheriff McGuire, though Glenn wasn't a sheriff back then. He was a student at UT. He kept telling me about this wonderful girl he was dating. Finally he brought her home for me and his parents to meet."

"And that was Mother?"

Troy smiled and nodded. "One look at her and I knew she was the woman I wanted to spend the rest of my life with. Her parents were against the marriage from the beginning. They were from Boston and hated that their beautiful Helene was going to settle for a poor cowboy."

"How did you get the money to purchase Willow Creek Ranch?"

"Your mother worked until Wyatt was born. We scrimped and saved part of the down payment. A good friend of mine named Able Drake backed me for the rest of it."

"Were you happy before the trouble started?"

"What trouble?"

"Whatever trouble drove you and Mother apart."

"Nothing drove us apart. Our love was as strong the day she was killed as it had ever been. The night before, we'd danced to music on the radio until past midnight. I can still remember how she'd fit in my arms."

Troy turned away, but not before Dakota glimpsed the moisture in his eyes. If he was faking the way he'd felt about Helene, he was doing a bang-up job of it.

"I loved your mother with all my heart. I can't control what you believe, Dakota. But I won't apologize for sins you think I may have committed. Not here in this house where we made love and gave life to you boys. I won't have her memory tainted by misconceptions and lies."

His dad had a point, but the resentment that had festered inside Dakota for so many years wouldn't be abated by mere words. He knew that. Still, the questions persisted.

"I was six years old. Just a kid. Did you ever once think that it was your duty to make certain I was safe?"

"What are you saying, Dakota? Were you abused by your uncle?"

"It's a little late in the game to worry about that now. I just wondered if it ever crossed your mind that I was still your son and not a fruitcake that you could just pack off and mail to a distant family member who no one else in the family even talked to."

"Were you abused?" Troy persisted.

"Let it go, Dad. I'm a man now and Uncle Larry is dead. I no longer need a champion. I'd just like to hear your side of this."

Troy worried the scar on his face, tracing the jagged outline all the way to his breastbone. "Not a day went by that I didn't think about you, Dakota. I wasn't as close to any of you guys as your mother was. I admit that. I worked the ranch most days from sunup to sundown, trying to keep our heads above water. She spent a lot more time with you."

"So when Mother died, you just turned us over to her parents. Didn't you have a say in what happened to us? Couldn't you have made them keep us brothers together so that we could watch each other's backs?"

"I had no say. Your grandparents were granted custody by court order. I assumed at first they'd take all of you to live with them."

"Why would you assume that?"

"They were constantly begging Helene to leave me and take you boys to Boston so that they could give you the material things I couldn't. But then when your mother died, apparently your grandmother let the grief kill her."

"Was Mother leaving you?"

"To go back to Boston? No. Hell, no. Helene had gone to school at UT to escape her mother's dreams for her. Helene was beautiful. Your grandmother expected her to marry well and move up the societal ladder in the way she hadn't been able to do herself.

"Helene wanted no part of Boston. She loved the ranch. She loved me. Most of all, she loved you boys. You were the center of her life, especially you, Dakota. You were her baby." Troy smiled. "I took you with me whenever I could just to keep her from spoiling you even more than she already had."

That pretty much summed it up. His mother would have kept him safe, but his mother was dead. No matter how Troy dressed it up, the truth was more likely that nobody but Uncle Larry would take the spoiled brat of the family. Dakota had been thrown to the wolves.

"I know I let you down, Dakota. If I could go back and change things, I would. But the past is the past. The only thing I know to do to help make things right is to find your mother's killer. I swear I'll never give up until I do."

"I guess that about covers it," Dakota said.

It didn't change the past or the present. In fact it gave him surprisingly little satisfaction. Laying the blame at Troy's feet wasn't the end-all solution Dakota had always imagined it would be.

Troy picked up the plane and went back to the task Dakota had interrupted. "I'm making this horse for Briana. I know she's not old enough for it yet, but when she is, she'll have it. I can't get a do-over with my sons but I plan to be the best grandfather I can be. I want to enjoy every minute of it."

"I'm sure Briana will like the horse," Troy said. "Viviana will be thrilled with it. She's already claimed all of you as family."

"You have a precious daughter," Troy said. "You'll make some mistakes, but this is your chance to be the parent you wish I'd been. Go for it. And if you mess up with Viviana, then I have to say you're a damn fool."

And that might be the most significant piece of wisdom Dakota had ever gleaned from his father.

"YOU DON'T KNOW HOW much I hate making this call, Dr. Mancini, but we can't have a trial without a suspect. Hank Bateman can't be found, therefore the case against him has been removed from the court's docket indefinitely."

As soon as Viviana ended the conversation with Melody Hollister, she turned off her phone and tossed it onto the bed. She didn't need to hear anything else.

The threats. The gunman. The attempted break-in. The doll with the crushed head. Everything she'd endured was for nothing.

Tears of frustration filled her eyes. She had to get out of this house.

She should never have come here, never told Dakota that he had a daughter. He was too screwed up by his past to ever love her or Briana.

She wasn't doing that much better with her own stinking past. And now a fine pair she and Dakota had turned out to be. So hot for each other they sizzled and not enough sense to turn the heat into something sane and lasting.

She lifted Briana from her crib and went to look for Dakota. It was time for her and her daughter to go home. Alone. And Dakota could take his lack of closure and killer reputation to the bulls. She and Briana didn't need an emotional attachment with him.

PANIC WAS STARTING to buck inside Dakota by the time he finally found Viviana. She was sitting on a bale of hay just outside the horse barn, rocking back and forth and cradling Briana in her arms.

Briana was sucking her thumb and waving her plastic keys, seemingly oblivious to the tears that were rolling down Viviana's cheeks. He knew he'd upset her earlier, but he hadn't expected this.

He went and sat down by Viviana, half expecting her to slam him off her bale and knowing he deserved it. "Is this a private crying jag or can anyone join?"

"Don't lecture me."

"I wouldn't dare."

"Then you can stay."

He eased an arm around her shoulders.

"I always thought he hated me," Viviana said, "but you know what? He didn't. Hate would have required caring and he barely knew I existed."

Dakota was thoroughly confused. "Are we talking about anyone I know?"

"I'm talking about my miserable excuse for a father. My mother worked at least two jobs all her life just to make ends meet. He never worked one for more than a few weeks at a time. There was never even money for rent. That's why we had to move so often. Do you know how embarrassing it is to be evicted and have your friends see your clothes piled out on the street?"

"Can't say that I do." And even if he did, he wasn't getting into a childhood-horror contest with her. He could win that hands down.

"We never knew if he was coming home or not and then one day he didn't. Not just any day, mind you." The tears fell harder. "It was the day Mom was diagnosed with cancer."

Maybe he wouldn't win hands down.

Briana began to squirm. He took off his shirt and spread it over a grassy spot next to Viviana's hay bale. He took Briana from her and set her on the soft denim shirt.

Briana rolled onto her stomach and pushed up into a crouching position. "Ba ba ba a ga."

"You're welcome." Dakota resettled next to Viviana. "What brought this on? Did you hear from your father?"

Viviana buried her head in her hands. He

hugged her close while she sobbed. Finally, she sniffed a few times and wiped her eyes with the heels of her hands. "I don't know how my father got into this, except that I keep comparing him to your family."

Falling apart over nothing didn't sound like Viviana. "Is that the only thing that prompted the tears?"

"No. It's just the first time I've cried since right after my mother died, so I guess I just pulled out all the stops."

"What's really wrong, Viviana?"

She took a deep breath and exhaled as if she were blowing rings of smoke. "The trial has been postponed indefinitely. No suspect, no trial. Hank Bateman just walks free to kill again and then harass and intimidate witnesses so that no one will dare testify against him."

Dakota's muscles bunched into tight knots. He'd been mad when he'd wanted to kill George Bateman this morning. Now he was really pissed off.

Viviana had been through hell because she'd been determined to do the right thing. Dirty Harry had been shot. Kevin Lucas had been murdered. Some guy had been set on fire in Viviana's new car.

All likely connected to Hank Bateman. And those were just the crimes they knew about. Now the cops had let Hank Bateman slip through their hands. The trial for a killer had been postponed the way you might call a baseball game because of rain.

"Not this time." The words came out like curses.

"There's nothing we can do about it," Viviana said.

"Don't be so sure. I'm willing to bet George knows where Hank is. And I know where George lives."

"You're not confronting George again. It's too risky. That's police work."

"Then maybe I'll just have to give the cops a nudge."

Ideas filtered through his mind in rapid succession as they walked back to the ranch house. Only this time, he wouldn't go it alone. The first thing he'd do was call Wyatt.

All his brothers were strong, capable and eager to help. Wyatt was the only one who had the determination of a Ledger plus the experience of a big-city homicide detective.

And Dakota had the determination of a jackass. If the two of them worked together, how could they fail?

IT WAS EIGHT O'CLOCK before Wyatt returned Dakota's phone call. Dakota was on the porch having an after-dinner bourbon while the electric ceiling fan whirred monotonously above him.

"Sorry to be so late getting back to you, but I was at a grizzly crime scene when you called and just now got my messages. The criminals in this state are getting more brazen and just plain crazier every day."

"And getting away with murder," Dakota said.

"Not if we cops can help it. What's the latest with Viviana's situation?"

"Hank Bateman's given the cops the slip. As a result the trial has been postponed indefinitely."

"I was afraid of that when the judge let him out on that penny-ante bail. That made no sense. Unless…"

"Unless what?" Dakota questioned.

"Probably nothing. I tend to jump to the realm of bizarre possibilities. I guess Viviana and her daughter will be returning to San Antonio?"

"Do you think the danger's past?"

"It should be, but you can't be sure. Hank may figure he has a score to settle with Viviana. George may be looking to settle one with you. You know the routine."

"Actually, I don't. The villains in my life are mostly bulls."

"Best to keep it that way. Let the cops handle the Batemans."

"I like the odds better if at least one of the Batemans is in jail. I'm thinking of going after Hank myself."

"That's a very dangerous idea."

"Would you do it, if Viviana were your daughter's mother?"

"That's an unfair question. I'm a cop."

"Would you?"

"The truth?"

"Yeah."

"In a heartbeat."

"That's what I thought. I'm open to advice on how to apprehend Hank. I figure you know as much about that as anyone in this part of Texas."

"Let me think on it tonight. I'll call you first thing in the morning."

"I guess I can wait that long."

"In the meantime, don't let down your guard at the ranch. By now the Batemans may have figured out that's where you are."

"I wish Hank would show up here," Dakota said. "It would save me the trouble of tracking him down."

"Sleep with your gun loaded, one eye open and never underestimate the enemy. That's the first lesson in Survival 101."

"What's lesson two?"

"Sleep with your gun loaded, one eye open and never underestimate the enemy."

"Got it."

Dakota finished his bourbon and stared into the darkness. The night was eerily quiet and an oppressive layer of clouds had blacked out the illumination of the moon and stars.

An owl hooted from a branch of a nearby mesquite tree. Something rustled the grass beneath the thick thorny bushes near the driveway. A coyote howled in the distance.

Nothing unusual or alarming, but Dakota had an uneasy feeling as he went inside and locked the front door behind him. He'd definitely sleep with one eye open tonight…if he slept at all.

THE WIND PICKED UP, blowing dust into vicious whirlwinds that clogged Viviana's lungs and burned her eyes. She tried to run for the house but the dust was so thick she couldn't see to get her bearings.

She fell and her knee slammed against something with a sharp edge. Blood spurted in her face and sprayed the top of the casket. A tiny casket. A baby's casket.

She lifted the lid. Leslie Compton stared back at her accusingly.

The wind died and the sand fell to the earth like blood.

The air grew instantly frigid.…

Viviana opened her eyes. There was neither sand nor a casket, but shadowy veils floated about the room. The faint odor of summer flowers wafted on the icy breeze.

The ghost had returned, but this time Viviana wasn't afraid.

"I know you're worried about Dakota, Helene. I'm worried about him, too. I love him just as you do, but I can't reach him."

The veils began to crackle. The figure of a woman materialized in the fog.

"Time is running out. Danger is near."

"Danger to whom? Dakota? Briana? Me? You have to tell me, Helene. You have to help me save us all."

The figure floated toward the glass doors that opened to the garden. The veils followed.

"Follow your heart, my dear. Follow your heart."

Blistering heat suffused the room. Viviana kicked off the sheet and jumped from the bed. This time she didn't bother with the robe.

Her bare feet were all but soundless on the polished hardwood floors. She paused at Dakota's door for only an instant before she opened it and stepped inside.

"Viviana." Dakota jerked to a sitting position. "Is something wrong?"

"Yes. But it's time to make it right." She unbuttoned her freshly laundered nightshirt and let the soft pink cotton pool at her feet. She stood in front of him naked, exposed in every way.

Then she slid beneath the sheet and into Dakota's waiting arms.

QUESTIONS AND DOUBTS exploded in his brain. Viviana silenced them with the touch of her lips to his.

Desire coursed through him so instantly and completely that he forgot everything except the thrill of Viviana. He kissed her, ravaging her lips while the excitement she incited reached every part of his body.

She reacted with the same delirious passion and brazen inhibition that she had before. Her hands tangled in his hair as she slid her tongue between his lips. They kissed until his lungs burned for air.

He wanted her all the way and all at once, but he forced himself to slow down. He kissed her mouth, her eyelids, her nose, then laid her on her back so that he could taste and explore every inch of her beautiful body.

Kicking out of his boxers, he trailed kisses down the smooth column of her neck to her perfect breasts. Her hand slid between their bodies, touching her most private parts and then massaging her slick moisture onto his throbbing erection.

"You make it difficult to go slow," he whispered.

"Then don't. Take me the way you did before, as if you'd never get enough of me."

"I never did. And I haven't wanted anyone since."

"Nor have I, so we can forget protection."

"What about getting pregnant?"

"I'm on the pill. I held on to the dream that you'd come back one day and want the same things I did. That all you'd need was me and Briana."

He pulled away. "I can't give you…"

She kissed the protests from his lips. "I'm not looking for forever tonight. I just need this moment and you."

"And I need you, more than you'll ever know."

Passion took over, whipping Dakota into a frenzy of desire so intense he couldn't hold back. He lifted himself over Viviana. She cradled his throbbing erection and guided it into her before wrapping her arms and legs around him.

Blood rushed to his head as he thrust deeper and deeper inside her. His heart pounded, his body exploded and Viviana rode with him straight over the top.

He held her close as the afterglow settled

over them. He'd thought she'd fallen asleep until she began to stir again. She kissed his stomach and twirled a finger inside his navel.

"Do you remember the night we got whipped cream and chocolate syrup all over my sheets?"

"And in my ear," Dakota said.

"And in my hair. All of my hair," Viviana teased. "It took three showers and half a bottle of shampoo to get it out."

"I remember," Dakota said. "I helped. Those were the top three showers of my life."

His body began to come alive again, probably a new record for recovery time.

Any thought of danger had moved to the back of his mind.

The sound of gunfire brought it crashing down on him again.

Chapter Sixteen

Dakota leaped from the bed and pulled on his jeans. "Lock yourself in Briana's room," Dakota ordered as he grabbed his gun.

There was more gunfire and the sound of breaking glass at the back of the house. Dakota raced down the hallway.

By the time he reached the kitchen, a man was lying facedown in a pool of blood. Troy was leaning over him, checking for a pulse. A rifle was propped against the chair next to him.

"Two of them were breaking into the house," Troy said. "The other son of a bitch got away." Blood wet Troy's left sleeve and trickled across his hand.

"You got hit."

"Friggin' flesh wound. That's all."

"Call an ambulance."

"Too late," Troy said. "This dude is dead."

"Call it for you. In the meantime, Viviana's a doctor. Just protect her and Briana while she tends to that arm."

"Take the deer rifle," Troy said. "It's loaded and more accurate at a distance."

Dakota exchanged weapons and left through the back door at a dead run. He spotted a pickup truck near the horse barn, picking up speed as it bounced and rocked along the rocky surface toward the ranch road.

He fired once and hit nothing.

Dylan's pickup roared toward him from the west and skidded to a stop next to him. "Get in."

"How the hell did you get here so fast?"

"I thought I heard something go past on the road near the house. Never saw lights. Called the guard. No answer. Decided to check it out myself. Heard gunfire and saw you."

He fired the explanation at the same speed he was driving—as fast as he could go. He quickly narrowed the distance between him and the escaping pickup truck.

Dakota lowered the window and pushed the gun outside. He'd never shot from a speeding vehicle before, but he took aim as best he could. There was a loud clunking sound as the first bullet ricocheted off the back fender of the truck they were chasing. The truck left the road, taking down a fence as it cut across the rolling pasture.

"Go for the tires," Dylan shouted.

"I was."

Dakota fired in rapid succession. One of the bullets finally took out a rear tire.

With one tire flat, the truck began to skid but didn't stop. Dakota reloaded and shot another round into the back of the truck, taking out the other tire.

The driver brought the truck to a jerky stop.

"Save your bullets," Dylan said. "We've got him now."

"And we need him alive," Dakota said. "The other one's dead."

"There's another one?"

"The one who shot Troy, but don't panic. Troy's injury is only a flesh wound. He's there with Viviana and Briana."

The man jumped from his truck and took off running toward a cluster of cedar trees. Dakota took off after him. The chest injury fired up again, and he felt as if he were breathing flames. He ran all the harder. He was not letting the guy get away.

He dived for the man football-style and managed to tackle him to the ground just before he reached tree cover. The man went for his gun.

Dylan arrived just in time to stamp the man's gun hand into the rocky earth. The pistol fell from his smashed fingers and Dylan kicked the weapon into the trees.

There was just enough light that Dakota could tell this was not Hank Bateman. He toed the man's arm. "Start talking."

"Keep your foot off me. I've got rights."

"Yeah. Try this *right* on for size." He propped the barrel of his rifle against the man's chest. "You have the right to start talking or I'll see if I can put a bullet right through the center of your heart."

"There wasn't supposed to be any trouble."

"What was there supposed to be?"

"I was told everyone would be asleep and we would just break in and abduct the doctor and her kid."

"Told by whom?"

"I said all I'm saying. I'm not naming names. I'm not that stupid."

Dakota poked his chest with the barrel of the rifle. "Who sent you?"

The guy shook his head. Dylan aimed his rifle at the man's head. "Let me have this one."

"Go ahead. He's no good to me. Take him out." Dakota turned as if he were ready to walk away and leave the guy with Dylan.

"Okay, okay," the man sputtered. "It was Hank Bateman who gave the orders."

"Are you a friend of Hank's?"

"Hank doesn't have friends."

"So what's your connection?"

"I owe him."

"For drugs?"

"Ask Hank."

"I'd love to. Where do I find him?"

"You could have found him right here on Willow Creek Ranch if you hadn't come after me. I'm sure he's finished taking care of his business and is long gone by now."

Damn. Hank had been on the spread and Dakota had missed his chance. Instead of guarding the place himself, he'd been in bed with Viviana.

Never underestimate your enemy.

He'd failed Survival 101.

So had his guards. They hadn't answered Dylan's call. They hadn't shown up at the first sound of gunfire.

Unless the guards had been Hank's business.

Dylan pulled out his cell phone and started punching in numbers.

"Who are you calling?" Dakota asked.

"My father-in-law. This is his turf and I think we need some local law enforcement on the scene."

"Agreed."

The call took less than a minute from beginning to end.

"McGuire and three deputies are driving onto the ranch right now," Dylan said.

"Where was he, sitting outside the gate waiting on you to call?"

"Collette called him the second I left the house. He was riding rounds with a new deputy tonight and they were in the area. He called in two more who were working a car break-in on Hutchens Road."

The gang was all here…after the fact.

Except that his hired guards were still unaccounted for. And Hank Bateman could be anywhere, regrouping for his next attack.

But why go to these extremes to silence a witness in a trial that wasn't going to be held?

Whatever the reason, Hank Bateman had to be stopped.

He was the bull that Dakota had to ride to the ground. The cost of failure could be Viviana's life.

THE COFFEE WAS STILL BREWING and the first rays of morning sun were painting golden squares on the kitchen table when Dakota's cell phone announced an incoming call from Wyatt.

"I just had a call from Dylan. He says Dad got shot last night during a rip-roaring, old-time western gun battle."

"Sadly, with a body count of two. Things have deteriorated fast since we spoke last night."

"Two? I thought I counted three when Dylan was giving the wrap-up."

"Our guard who took the knife to the gut is in the hospital but holding his own. The guard whose throat was sliced died on the scene. And the guy Dad shot through the window died from a piece of jagged glass that sliced through his windpipe."

"Tough way to go."

"So is having your throat slashed."

"How's Dad?"

"He had to have a few dozen stitches in his arm, and he'll have another scar to add to his collection, but he's fine. Already hollering to come home."

"Can't blame him. He's got a doctor staying in his house."

"A very upset doctor. Viviana thinks the deaths are her fault. She's lamenting that she came to the ranch."

"If she hadn't come there, she'd probably be dead."

"I know. I get sick just thinking about what Hank Bateman would have done to her and Briana if his henchmen had abducted them."

"Luckily Dad was awake and in the kitchen when they attempted the break-in, at least that's the way I heard it."

"That's the way Dad told it," Dakota said. "He said he woke from a sound sleep. He thought one of us had come to his room, but when he turned on the light to look, there was no one there. He went to the kitchen for a glass of water and saw the shadow of a guy as he skulked from that storage building out back toward the house."

"I heard Dad shot him with a rifle."

"He did. When he saw the shadow, he took the rifle from the locked case and waited until the guy was at the window. He didn't see the second guy until he took off running."

"And that was the guy you and Dylan chased down?"

"Right, the one who admitted Hank is behind all of this. So have you come up with ideas for locating Hank?"

"About that… I did some checking. You really don't want to get involved with him or his brother, Dakota."

"I don't have a choice."

"You do. Just give it some time and I think it will take care of itself."

"Why would you think that?"

"I shouldn't be telling you this so keep it under your hat. Both brothers are being investigated by the Feds. Arrests may be in the foreseeable future."

"Which also means arrests may not be made in the foreseeable future."

"True. I'm giving you the best scenario."

"Help me here," Dakota said. "How did

killing Leslie Compton became a federal case?"

"It didn't. The Feds are investigating them for something else altogether. The Batemans will get taken off the streets eventually and in the meantime, you don't want to become a statistic."

"I don't want Viviana or Briana becoming statistics, either."

"Then persuade Viviana to stay at the ranch awhile longer."

"Why are the Feds after them?"

"I can't talk about the case against them. I've already said more than I should have. They're in big trouble. Viviana is just fun and games for them and there won't be any more fun and games once they're arrested. So just give this some time."

"I appreciate the advice."

"I hope that means you're going to follow it."

"I'll give it some thought."

"Don't make me have to come down there."

"Why not? Then we'd have the whole gang down here."

"The sons of Troy Ledger ride again."

"Sounds like a movie title."

"Let's make it one with a happy ending, Dakota."

"Wouldn't have it any other way."

VIVIANA PLACED the stack of neatly folded panties in the suitcase. Briana reached over and pulled them out.

"I know you don't want to leave the ranch, sweetheart, but we have to. Mama is trouble, trouble, trouble."

"Ma-ma. Ma-ma."

"You said it! You said 'Mama.' On the day I needed good news the most." Viviana picked up Briana and hugged her tight.

Dakota stopped in the doorway. "Did I hear shouting in here?"

"Briana just said 'Mama.' Say it again, sweetie. Mama. Mama."

"Ab a ca oo."

"Well, she said it twice, so that means it wasn't just an accident," Viviana said.

"I'm not doubting you." Dakota stepped into the room. "Why are you packing? Are we going somewhere?"

"I'm going away for a while."

"Going where?"

"To California."

"That's not just another state. It's another world from Texas."

"I appreciate everything you've done, Dakota, but I can't keep living in this constant state of flux and I certainly can't expect it of your family."

"Coming here was your idea."

"Yes, and it seemed to make sense when we were talking about a week at the most, but this is a nightmare with no termination date."

"When did you plan to tell me this?"

"When I finished packing. I have a car coming to pick me up at eleven and I have a flight from Austin to Los Angeles at two-thirty this afternoon."

"Do you have a place to stay in L.A.?"

"One of my friends from med school is there. She says the hospitals out there need emergency medicine specialists and that I'll have no trouble getting a job. Briana and I can stay with her until I find a place of my own."

"I don't blame you for giving up on me as a protector. I've failed you miserably, but don't you think quitting your job is going a bit too far?"

"You didn't fail me or Briana. We're both

safe. It's just that keeping us safe has become too costly and dangerous for everyone around me."

"No one wants you to leave the ranch."

"They should be demanding it. Two men are dead. Another may not make it. Your father is in the hospital. And what if Hank had stopped at Dylan's and sliced his and Collette's throats? Do you think I could ever live with myself after that?"

He walked over and took her free hand. "Look, Viviana, I admit that this isn't working, but we'll come up with another plan."

"You have bulls to ride."

"Three more days. Give me three more days to come up with a plan. If I don't have one by then, L.A. will still be there." He leaned over and kissed her.

Briana grabbed his nose, making the kiss more of a challenge than an act of passion. Still, it took her breath away.

Her cell phone rang. She checked the caller ID. "It's Shelby Lucas."

"I'll take Briana while you talk, but put the phone on speaker so I can hear what she has to say."

Briana put her short, chubby arms around

Viviana's neck as she tried to pass her to Dakota. Somehow he managed to charm her into letting go.

Viviana dropped to the side of the bed and switched the phone to speaker. "Hello."

"Hi. This is Shelby. We talked at the restaurant."

"Yes, I remember you well. You're Hank Bateman's girlfriend."

"I *was* his girlfriend."

"Did you break up with him since we talked?"

"He dumped me for that slut Karen Compton."

"Leslie's mother?"

"Right. I found out he's been seeing her ever since he got out of jail."

Surely Karen hadn't gone back to Hank after he'd killed her baby, but then Viviana shouldn't be that shocked at anything that happened in Hank's world.

"Why are you calling, Shelby?"

"I overheard Hank talking to George. He's planning to kill you and your baby. There's been too much killing. That's why I wanted to warn you."

"Why would he kill me?"

"To make you pay for calling the police on him and saying he killed Karen's baby."

"I only reported the cause of death. The police connected Hank to the death on their own."

"Whatever. I thought with him wanting to kill you and all, you might want to know where Hank is hiding."

Dakota motioned to Viviana and whispered instructions.

"Yes. I'd love to know where Hank is."

"It's an abandoned house in a wooded area near the river. I can't tell you where it is, but I can show you. You might want to take that cowboy with you. He's not afraid of anything, not even George. He's a good shot, too."

"Why didn't you go to the cops with this information?"

"I don't deal with cops. If I show you and that cowboy where Hank is, you have to promise no cops."

"What do you have against cops?"

"It's what they have against me."

"Warrants for your arrest?"

"Yeah. For writing bad checks, shoplifting.

Stuff like that. Nothing big. I'm calling 'cause I want to help you, Dr. Mancini. But it's also because I need money real bad."

"So you expect me to pay you for showing me this house in the woods?"

"One thousand dollars in twenties. That's enough for me to get back to Mississippi. I've got family there. But you have to show up with the cowboy even if you don't go after Hank with us. I have to know you're in on this. I trust you not to tell the cops."

Dakota nodded his approval but this sounded like a trap to Viviana.

"I can meet you at that same restaurant where we met before," Shelby said. "Can you make it by three o'clock this afternoon?"

"I haven't agreed to anything yet."

"Okay, but if you want to get Hank before he kills you, bring the money to the restaurant at three. I'll be parked near the front entrance so you won't even have to go inside. If you're not there, that's okay, too. I'm leaving town with or without the money. I'm tired of getting pushed around by the Batemans."

Shelby broke the connection before Viviana could give her an answer.

"I'll be there," Dakota said, as if Shelby could hear him.

"I don't trust her," Viviana said. "This is either a trap or just a ploy to get cash."

"Maybe it's not a trap. Hell hath no fury like a woman scorned, you know."

"A woman whose fury can be lessened with a thousand dollars."

"I'll make sure that I'm ready for any trick she might try. I just have a few details to work out. I'll have the sheriff and his deputies come out and stay with you and Briana. He's offered to help in anyway he can."

"Not so fast," Viviana said. "If you're determined to meet with Shelby, I'm going with you. Collette, Dylan and her sheriff father can take care of Briana."

"No. You said yourself that this could be a trap."

"I'm the one Shelby trusts, Dakota. I'll see if Collette will watch Briana while we're away."

"You're not going, Viviana. Final answer."

"It's either the flight to Los Angeles or the steak restaurant. You decide."

"Did anyone ever tell you you're a hardheaded woman?"

"All the time, and thank you."

He kissed her again, slower, sweeter, wetter than before. Briana bit him on the nose.

"Be ready at one," he said and then turned and walked away.

WHEN THEY WERE within fifteen minutes of arriving at the restaurant, Dakota made one last call to Detective Gordon Miles to make certain that the details of the plan were in place.

"Everything's a go," the detective assured him. "I'm parked across the street in an unmarked car. You won't see me en route, but I'll stay just close enough that I don't lose you."

"What about the guard for Viviana?"

"Sergeant Blake will keep her in his sights. He'll pull in front of the restaurant exactly five minutes after we pull out, also in an unmarked car and wearing street clothes."

"How will Viviana recognize him?"

"He'll be driving a dark blue Ford Taurus and wearing jeans and a blue polo shirt. He'll stop near the front door of the restaurant, get out and put a black laptop bag in the backseat of the car. That will be her signal that it's safe to get in the car. Then they'll go to her town house and wait for you to come back for her."

"At that point, you should have Hank Bateman in custody," Dakota said.

"If all goes as planned."

Dakota pulled to a stop at a red light. The restaurant was just ahead. "Have you heard anything new on Harry Cortez's condition?"

"Yes, good news. He not only started talking today but he's also finally making sense."

"Did he ID his shooter?"

"Yep. Guess who?"

"Hank Bateman."

"You got it. I hope to go by the hospital tonight and tell him Bateman is locked up and that we threw away the key. Even better news would be that we had to shoot the bastard in self-defense."

The light turned green. Dakota pulled across the intersection. "Any luck yet with identifying the man who was burned in Viviana's car?"

"Also just in. His name is Ronnie Pellor. He was a stoolie for one of our narcotics agents, same as Kevin Lucas was. I'm sure one of the traffickers put out a hit on them."

Dakota hadn't heard that about Kevin

Lucas but it would explain why Detective Cortez didn't admit knowing who Kevin was referring to when he'd muttered "Shell." The cops protected pigeons.

"I'm pulling into the restaurant parking lot now," Dakota said.

"I've got you spotted."

"Shelby's parked near the front entrance just as she said she'd be," Dakota said.

"In the red Jeep?"

"Yep.

"I figured that was her."

"Looks like she may be sporting some new bruises," Dakota said, "though it's hard to tell from here."

"She pulled a gun on George Bateman the other day," Miles said. "I'm sure that didn't earn her flowers. Now, remember, make sure the backseat and the trunk are empty before you get in or hand over any money. And keep your pistol ready, just in case Shelby's packing and lying."

"Got it," Dakota said. "See you in the little house in the big woods."

"And here's hoping we also see Hank."

SHELBY DROVE AT LEAST ten miles over the speed limit, recklessly switching lanes and barely avoiding a collision with a semi. She surfed the radio channels every time a song finished until she finally settled on a heavy rock station that played nothing Dakota would consider music.

"You seem nervous," Dakota noted, baiting as much as questioning. His suspicions of this being a trap were growing stronger with each mile they traveled.

"Wouldn't you be nervous if you were ratting out Hank Bateman?"

"Probably. Is he the one who did that to your face?"

"Do you recognize his artistic touches?"

"Just a lucky guess." He looked out the window, then back to Shelby.

"How did you learn Hank's location?"

"I've got my ways of finding out things," Shelby said.

Yep. He was being driven into a trap, but this time he and Detective Miles would be ready for whatever surprises Hank threw their way. At least he hoped they would.

Thirty minutes after they'd left the restaurant, Shelby stopped the car at the end of a deserted road. Beyond them was a thick wooded area. There was no sign of the detective.

Dakota was starting to get a tad nervous.

"I don't see a house," he said.

"We took the back roads. You can't see it from here but it's about a ten-minute walk through the woods. Just stay east of the tree line. You can't miss it."

"I thought you were here to show me the way."

"I'll stay here with the car. When I see you coming, I'll start the engine for a fast getaway."

He waited. There should be some sign of the detective by now.

"Are you going to get out or not?" Shelby asked, clearly impatient.

"I'm thinking about it." He lowered the window. The air was hot and humid. A murder of loud crows darted in and out of the branches of a scrawny oak tree. A lone butterfly fluttered among the honeybees sipping nectar from the honeysuckle vines that climbed a nearby fence.

There was a whir in the distance, growing louder as it came closer. Maybe a motorbike. Dakota opened the car door and stepped out, his hand resting on the butt of his gun.

He was usually comfortable trusting his instincts, but they seemed off-kilter today.

He caught sight of movement in the trees. Could be a deer but Dakota figured it was Hank.

"Afternoon, Ledger." George Bateman stepped into the clearing, his pistol pointed at Dakota. "You just can't stay away from me, can you?"

The sound of gunfire blasted through the still air. Crows scattered in every direction. The gun George had been holding fell from his hands and at least ten men in SWAT suits surrounded him.

Detective Miles drove up and stepped out of his car. "Good work, Dakota."

"Thanks. Now would someone mind telling me what the devil's going on?"

Shelby gunned her engine and threw the car into Reverse.

"Let her go," Miles called loudly enough for everyone to hear. "She's small potatoes. We can pick her up anytime."

Miles walked over to where Dakota stood as two helicopters landed a few feet from the tree line.

"This is a federal operation that's been in

the work for months," Miles explained, yelling over the helicopters' roar. "They finally got the evidence they needed to tie George and Hank to several dozen cartel-related murders over the past two years. That's why the judge agreed to set bail for Hank so close to the trial. They needed a few more pieces of evidence that Hank conveniently led them to."

"I still don't get it."

"It's kind of a trade-off. They arrest Hank and hope for him to provide info to catch one of the big guys who's ordering hits on police officers all along the border."

"And George?"

"He's a worker bee. He does as he's told, but he's not connected the way Hank is. Up until he was arrested for Leslie Compton's murder, Hank was moving into the upper echelon of one of the biggest cartels."

"And he blew all that by killing his girlfriend's baby. He doesn't sound that smart to me."

"I'm sure he never thought he'd go to jail."

"Because he and George would intimidate the witnesses. I'm still not sure why you included me in any of this."

"The Feds have been searching for Hank for two days. Every time they think they have him cornered, he fools them. You called and offered to deliver. The Feds decided to take you up on it."

"The house is empty," someone yelled. "There's no sign of Hank."

Gordon Miles muttered a string of curses a mile long. "He's slipped through our fingers again." The detective went toward his men.

Dakota leaned against Miles's unmarked car. All this and no Hank Bateman. So where was he? Apprehension settled like lead in Dakota's gut. He took out his phone and called Viviana.

No answer.

He tried the number again, letting it ring until it switched to her voice mail.

This wasn't like her, not when she believed that Dakota might be walking into a trap.

He scanned the area, searching for the detective. Miles was nowhere in sight and there was no time to waste looking for him.

Dakota opened the door to the detective's car. The keys were in the ignition. That was all the invitation he needed.

VIVIANA SERVED A CUP of the fresh-brewed coffee to Sergeant Blake. "Feel free to turn on the television over the counter," she said, "or you can watch the one in the living room."

"No, I'm good. I like to keep my mind on the job."

"Do I have to sit with you or is it okay if I go upstairs?"

"You have full run of the house. I've already checked inside every closet, under every bed and even looked inside those two big chests you have at the end of the hall."

"In that case I think I'll go upstairs and lie down until Dakota gets back. I got very little sleep last night."

"Do whatever you want. If you need me, I'll be right here."

"Help yourself to more coffee whenever you want it."

"Yes, ma'am."

She did try resting, but she was so nervous she couldn't even close her eyes. Dakota and the detective had both assured her that nothing could go wrong this afternoon, but she couldn't get last night out of her mind.

In a matter of minutes two men had been killed and Troy had been wounded.

She needed this to be over. They all did. She couldn't think beyond that.

She went to the bathroom and washed her face. When she turned off the water, she heard a noise as if the detective had dropped something. She went to the head of the stairs and looked down.

"Are you all right?"

The house was deathly quiet.

"Sergeant Blake?"

The lack of a response and the quiet set her nerves on edge. She had to settle down. The officer was likely in the bathroom or checking something in the garage.

She took the stairs slowly, stopping on the landing to call again.

"Sergeant Blake? Are you in the kitchen?"

This time she heard whispered voices.

The television. He must have changed his mind about it and turned it low so as not to disturb her. She hurried into the kitchen. The sergeant was in the same chair as she'd left him.

Only now his hands were duct taped behind his back and his eyes were rolled back in his head as if he were drugged...or dead. A bloody knife lay next to him and there was a jagged cut down one arm. The blood had soaked into his uniform.

Chapter Seventeen

Viviana's heart pounded fiercely against the wall of her chest, the fear so strong her feet refused to move. Hank Bateman was somewhere inside the house. And not alone. She'd heard voices. Male and female. And he must have heard her calling.

He'd stayed out of sight, intentionally playing a vicious game of cat and mouse, no doubt delighting in her horror at the sight of the sergeant in her kitchen.

She checked Sergeant Blake's pulse. It was weak but not in the danger zone. She tiptoed past him and pulled a clean, bloodless chef's knife from the block on the counter.

"I know you're here, Hank. I know you see me."

There was still no response.

Holding the knife in her hand, she began

to tiptoe toward the back door. If she could just get outside, she could run and scream for help.

Her left hand was on the doorknob, the right still clutching the knife when she felt the sharp point of a blade prick the skin at the base of her skull.

"It's too early to leave, Dr. Mancini. The party is just beginning."

He'd sneaked up behind her, which meant he'd been hiding in the laundry room. But for how long? She was sure the sergeant had checked that room when they'd come in.

He wrapped his right hand around hers. "I'll take that knife before you hurt yourself and rob me of the pleasure."

She tried to swing her arm backward and hit him with the sharp blade. If she could just buy time the way she had with the key in the E.R. parking lot, she'd have at least a chance of escape.

He was too strong for her. He crushed her hand in his until she screamed from the pain and the knife clattered to the floor.

"How did you get in?" she asked.

He slid the point of the knife up and down

her neck, drawing beads of blood that slid down her flesh.

"It's quite easy to pick a lock when you know how, but this time I climbed in through the kitchen window."

"I don't believe you. Sergeant Blake would have heard you before you could get inside."

"That's why I came early. I knew I'd have plenty of time since Shelby wasn't meeting you until three."

He'd put Shelby up to this, which meant Dakota had surely walked into a trap. Her stomach began to roll.

"You made Shelby do this, didn't you?"

"Yes, the scared, fearful little dimwit is disgustingly easy to manipulate."

"She's in love with you."

"She's pregnant with my brother's child. They deserve each other. Karen, come in here. The doctor needs someone to help her undress before we practice our surgery."

"If you hurt me, Dakota Ledger and his brothers will hunt you down and cut out your heart."

"They may hunt, but they won't find me." Hank led her toward the table as Karen Compton joined them in the kitchen.

"Start with the blouse. I'll watch and decide where we should cut first."

Hank took a step away from her, removing the knife from her flesh for the first time since he'd come into the kitchen. But he was close enough that she'd never be able to get away before he caught her. She had to think, had to find a way to escape.

Karen's hands shook as she slipped the first pearl button of Viviana's blouse through the hole. Hank had claimed Shelby was easily manipulated. Perhaps Karen was, too.

Viviana put her mouth close to Karen's ear. "How can you stay with a man who killed your baby girl?"

Karen moved on to the next button, but now her hands were shaking so badly, she was having difficulty maneuvering the button through the hole.

"Your baby girl is dead," Viviana whispered. "She is gone from you forever. Hank did that to you."

Karen stepped away from Viviana. "Stop. Make her stop, Hank."

"No more talk of babies, Doc, or I'll skip right over the fun part."

"Baby killer," Viviana whispered.

Karen shoved Viviana into the table. "Hank didn't kill my baby. He didn't, so stop saying that. I killed her. Me. Her mother. She wouldn't stop crying. All day, all night, she just wouldn't stop. And then finally she did."

Karen fell to the floor sobbing.

Hank kicked Karen in the stomach. "I should have let you go to jail for killing that kid and then I wouldn't have to listen to your constant wailing about it."

He took the knife and sliced Viviana's blouse down the front so that it gaped open. Then he fit the blade inside her bra and sliced through it.

"Does that make you feel like a man?"

"I am a man. And you can shut up, too."

"Why should I do what you say when you're going to kill me no matter what I do? You're a monster, Hank, a certifiable beast. How does anyone ever get to be as heartless and evil as you are?"

He rolled the point of the knife across her nipples. "I'll tell you how, sweetheart. You have a dad who gets drunk two or three times a week and comes home and beats the living crap out of you. And if you whimper, he hits you that much harder. If you cry, he pokes you with his lit cigarette until you pass out from the pain."

Viviana backed up slowly as he talked, finally getting close enough to reach the bloody knife Hank had used on the cop. She picked it up and threw it at Hank, blade first. It impaled his chest and he stumbled backward. She dashed past him and ran for the door.

Hank grabbed her from behind, the knife still in his chest.

"Don't kill her," Karen begged. "She just wanted to help our baby."

"If you say one more word, I'll kill you, too."

He knocked Viviana to the floor then straddled her, holding her down with his knees while he yanked the knife from his bloodied chest and then held it to her throat.

One swipe across her jugular and she'd bleed to death.

She didn't want to die. She wanted to raise Briana. She wanted to hold tight to Dakota and love him.

She closed her eyes and thought of her cowboy and her baby while she waited for the sharp, quick slice of death.

Chapter Eighteen

"Answer the phone, Viviana. Please answer the phone and tell me I'm going crazy for nothing. Tell me you are sitting there drinking a diet soda while you entertain the cop with stories of life in the real E.R."

The phone switched to her voice-mail message once again. He didn't bother to leave one this time.

Dakota had made a grave error in judgment. He'd thought he had everything under control, but once again he'd underestimated the enemy.

He parked a few doors down from Viviana's town house. He'd circle the house first and try to assess what was going on inside. Play it smart and not just burst in and get shot before he could save Viviana.

He cut through the neighbor's yard and

slipped through the hedges to the bay window in front of the house. The living room was empty. Creeping as stealthily as he could, he skirted the side of the house and moved to the back. He stayed low as he neared the kitchen window.

Finally, he straightened and looked inside. The first thing he saw was the cop, his head rolled back, blood rolling off his chin and down his neck like a gaudy ruby necklace.

His heart plunged when he spotted Viviana. She was on the floor, her eyes closed, with Hank Bateman pressing a bloody kitchen knife to her throat.

Hank looked up, saw Dakota watching and threw back his head and laughed. Fury exploded like a bomb inside Dakota, and adrenaline coursed through his veins in angry waves. But this time he couldn't just act on impulse. This time it was Viviana's life on the line.

"So glad you made it in time to watch her die, Dakota. But if you make one move toward us, I'll have to kill her so fast it won't be fun for either of us."

A woman who seemed to materialize from

thin air walked over to Hank. She was holding a knife to her own throat.

"I'll die with you, Viviana. I killed my baby. I don't deserve to live."

Hank reached up to grab the knife from her hand. When he did, Viviana rolled from beneath him.

Dakota flew into action. He ripped off the screen with one quick jerk and smashed the butt of his pistol through the glass.

His gaze met Hank's for one split second before Dakota pulled the trigger and fired.

Hank fell back, dead before he hit the ground, thanks to a bullet between the eyes.

Heart pounding, Dakota climbed through the window, crossed the room and dropped to the floor beside Viviana. He took her into his arms and pulled her to him.

"I should never have left you," he said, "should never have trusted anyone to watch over you but me."

"You're here now, Dakota. You're here now and you have never looked or felt so good."

"And then what happened?" Collette asked.

Viviana sipped her ice-cold diet soda. "Detective Miles showed up. He'd come to the same realization that Dakota had about the time he looked up and saw Dakota speeding away in his unmarked vehicle."

"When he couldn't reach Blake, he called me," Dakota said. "He called for backup but by the time they arrived at Viviana's the ambulance had already picked up Blake and Hank Bateman. There was nothing for them to do but arrest Karen for assisting Hank in today's assault."

"And for the death of her daughter nearly a year ago," Viviana added, "though I don't think there's any punishment they can give her that is worse than the one she's given herself."

"How did you find out she was the one who killed the baby and not Hank?" Troy asked.

"She admitted it to me before Hank kicked her and long before my hero here showed up on the scene."

"It doesn't quite add up," Troy said. "Hank was a ruthless, heartless killer yet he took the blame for the baby's murder when it was Karen who killed her."

"Maybe he really loved her in his own way," Collette said.

"If that's love," Dylan said, "I hope to never have any part of it."

"I feel the same," Viviana said. "Now if you'll all excuse me, I need to check on Briana and then go to bed. I'm cratering fast."

Viviana got ready for bed first and then spent long minutes staring at Briana, grateful that she'd stayed alive to come home to her tonight. Helene Ledger had once faced a killer in this very house, but she hadn't tucked her kids in bed that night or ever again.

No wonder her spirit lingered and still worried for her boys.

When Viviana returned to the guest room, Dakota was standing at the glass door staring out at the courtyard garden his mother had loved so much.

"I'm glad it's finally over," he said. "I never want to be as afraid again as I was when I saw that knife at your throat."

"I was afraid, too. I wasn't ready to die. Now I'm more than ready to live my life to the fullest. But I can't help but feel just a little sad for Hank Bateman when I think of the way he grew up. Can you imagine being beaten almost daily by the one who should be keeping you safe?"

"I don't have to imagine it. I lived it."

Viviana's insides quaked at the sadness in Dakota's voice. She walked over and put her arms around his waist and rested her face against his back. "Do you want to talk about it?"

"I thought I wanted to. I thought I wanted to throw my past in the face of everyone in my family and punish them for letting me suffer at Uncle Larry's hands. It turns out I don't."

"What changed your mind?"

"Finding you again. Becoming a father. Meeting my family. All of the above in differing measures. When my mother died, life changed for all of us. None of us will ever get back what we lost. For me it was growing up without ever feeling safe."

"That must have made for a frightening childhood."

"It did. The only thing I loved growing up was the rodeo. That was my escape. It was pain with a purpose."

"Now I understand why you love it so much."

"I'm not sure about that but it may have

kept me from turning out like Hank Bateman."

"Or it might have been the six years of your mother's love that saved you."

Dakota put an arm around her shoulder. "I've been thinking a lot these past few days and I've made a couple of major decisions, Viviana."

"It may have been the stress," Viviana suggested cautiously. "Perhaps you should wait to tell me until you're sure the changes are what you really want."

"I'm sure now. I want us to be a real family. You, me and Briana. I want wedding bells, cake and a gold band. I'm ready to go whole hog. That is if you'll have me."

"What about bull riding?"

"If that's what it takes to be a family, I'll give that up, too."

"No. I've changed my mind about a few things, too. You can keep your bull riding. All it takes for us to be a family is love. But I would like that wedding you mentioned."

"Any kind of wedding you want—as long we have whipped cream and chocolate for the honeymoon."

Viviana melted into Dakota's arms and into

his kiss, sure she'd never been this happy in her life.

She lingered at the door to the garden after Dakota released her.

Hold on tight to Dakota. If you let go of him, he will be lost forever.

"I have him, Helene," she whispered. "You can let go now and rest in peace. But I didn't save Dakota. Love saved us both."

"Did you say something?"

"I said let's go to bed. I can't wait to sleep in your arms tonight and forever." Her forever had just turned to pure gold.

* * * * *

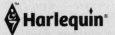